Black Tide

Blackstone, Volume 8

Rachel E Rice

Published by Rachel E Rice, 2023.

Black Tide
Book 8
By Rachel E Rice
Copyright by Rachel E Rice 2020
Re-edited in 2023

Copyright

Copyright 2020 by Rachel E. Rice

All rights reserved. No part of this book may be used or reproduced in any manner whatsoever without written permission, except in the case of brief quotations embodied in critical articles or reviews. Please do not participate in or encourage the piracy of copyrighted materials in violation of the author's rights. Purchase only authorized editions.

This is a work of fiction. Names, characters, places, and incidents are the product of the author's imagination. Any resemblance to actual persons, living or dead, events, or locales is entirely coincidental. No reproduction of this book part or whole is permitted. This book should not be scanned, or distributed in any printed or electronic form without the author's permission.

Also by Rachel E Rice

Blackstone

The Incredible Mr. Black

Blackstone Complete 10 Books Dark Romance Series

Temptation In Black

Blackstone Series 4 Books Box Set

Submission To Black

Black Tie Affair

The Incredible Mr. Black Box Set

Mourning Becomes Black

Fade To Black

Back to Black

Black Tide

Black Swan

Blackout

Blackstone Series 6 Books Box Set

I Am The Night

I Am The Night

Insatiable

Insatiable: The Lone Werewolf finds his mate
Insatiable: A Werewolf's Hunger
Insatiable: A Werewolf's Wedding
Insatiable: The Werewolves' Challenge
Hunter's Moon
Moon Tide
Moon Rapture

Insatiable Werewolf Series
A Bride For A Werewolf: The Beginning
Thorn in Moonscape
Insatiable: Damon in Moonscape
A Werewolf's Passion
Moonscape Box Set

Night
I Am First Night
I Am Last Night

Obsession
Obsession: Warm Bodies,Cold Hearts
Naked Obsession
Burning Obsession

Seduction
Seduced By An Earl

The Captain
The Captain and The Virgin

The Soul of A Vampire
Soul of A Vampire
Soul of A Vampire Book 2
Soul of A Vampire Book 3

To kill a vampire
To Kill a Vampire
To Kill A Vampire
To Kill A Vampire

Standalone
Finding Summer
One Desire
Insatiable Box Set: Books 1-4
Hunter's Moon Box Set
Hunter's Moon Insatiable Series
Insatiable: Tracker #8
Soul of A Vampire Box Set
The Complete Insatiable Werewolf Bundle
The Complete Insatiable Werewolf Bundle
I Am The Night Box Set
A Vampire Bundle
A Vampire Bundle

I Am The Night Box Set
To Kill A Vampire Boxset
To kill A Vampire Boxset
A Complete Vampire Bundle

Watch for more at www.rachel-e-rice.com.

Table of Contents

Chapter 1

Maximillian Blackstone wore an expression that Alex couldn't identify. What was it she saw on his face? Alex had never seen that look in his eyes before. Was it lust, love, jealousy, or hatred? She had to get close to him to find out. But she couldn't with Jonas lying as if in a coma. Hell, he'd had a terrible few days. A new wife on their wedding day killed. Not just killed, but her throat had been cut by her lover. Her disinterested parents, and not to mention a house full of police threatening to take him to the police station and arrest him if he didn't get out of town—immediately.

How much time did they give Jonas, Alex didn't know, but what she did know was Jonas had to go somewhere soon, but where?

By the look on Max's face his twin brother wasn't welcome back into their family since he'd walked into the unlocked house to see Alex and Jonas asleep in the same bed with Jonas clutching Alex to his chest.

Never mind that they both were clothed. Never mind that Alex never looked at Jonas in any way sexual, but as a tragic figure that she had to protect, and now she would have to protect him against the man he loved and respected the most—his brother, Max.

Looking up at Max, Alex felt a surge of desire that she'd never felt before. She touched his face with a warm palm and knowing glance. She knew what he desired, even if he didn't want to admit to it. It was sexual and it was hot.

Max stepped back as if he'd been touched by fire, and maybe he had. That fire had always burned bright between them even now that they had children, however, they'd never been this far apart before, and Alex had never felt a distance from Max until now. She had to bring him back because she didn't like the unusual glower in his eyes.

She wanted the warmth he'd always exhibited toward her. She wanted to feel his shaft, so she moved her hand downward, her fingers sliding down his muscular chest, down past his waist to palm his cock, but Max pinned her in place with his cold eyes.

This was a first.

Never had she been discouraged when it came to Max and sex. She moved closer to him where her body was flush against his, where she could smell the scent of his body, and he could smell hers too.

They were like two animals in heat every time they were near each other. He stared down at her, and his wide impressive chest moved up and down as his breathing grew stronger and more intense.

Without Alex knowing or approving, Max whisked her into his arms. She gazed into his cool eyes, and questioned, "Where are you going with me?" He headed down the hall and kicked open a guest room, brought Alex to the bed, and dropped her in it without a word.

"Take off your clothes or I will rip them off your body," he barked.

Had he planned on punishing her for being in the bed with Jonas, she didn't know. She just did as he requested as quickly as possible.

Alex thought that maybe this would save her marriage, because she understood how Max felt about her. She assumed he'd become excited and aroused by the sight of finding her and Jonas sleeping together.

Maybe that had his cock as hard as it was when she touched it.

Alex knew how jealous Max was, and maybe she could use that jealous nature to arouse him to a point that he wouldn't want to lose her, and give her time to explain about the misunderstanding. She knew if she could tell him her side of the story and he had time to mull over it, he would laugh about what had happened, and she would be back with him and her children.

Alex thought about protecting Jonas as well, and maybe Max would welcome him back once he'd realized what Jonas had gone through, and all this was just an innocent mistake. Surely Max wouldn't be so heartless as to send Jonas away.

She'd been in Jonas's arms through no fault of her own. He'd been drunk, and when he fell across the bed with his arms wrapped tightly around Alex she couldn't pry them from her. She'd been forced to fall with him on to the bed where he kept her in his tight grip as he slept, and eventually she'd fallen asleep as well, and Max walked into an open house to find them together in the same bed.

This wasn't my fault, she thought, *and neither was it Jonas's.* Max had to understand this, but she couldn't tell him now. Now when she lay naked in front of him with him ready to claim what was obviously his.

It wasn't Alex's fault, and it wasn't Jonas's fault, it was the fault of the circumstances that they found each other at the crossroads of their lives, and for Max to find them together the way he had, it had to have been a sign, but what sign was that?

She didn't believe in divine intervention.

Alex and Jonas thought Max had died in a plane crash, and they were inconsolable. The only support they had was with each other. After all, they were family, and the only ones left in the Blackstone family were Jonas, Alex, and Max's children. They thought that was all that was left of their small family because the head of that family had been assumed to be dead.

What more could Max expect? What more could he want from her? Max's searing sexy voice broke through her thoughts.

"Turn on your stomach," Max said with a low breathless dominant voice. "I want to look at you," Max insisted as his hand caressed her smooth porcelain skin. She turned hurriedly as he had requested.

Then Alex felt the sting from his palm, and the pain and heat coursing through her body arousing her. She wouldn't cry out or say a word, because she knew Max needed to get out his frustrations and hurt, so she gave in to the violent way he spanked her ass.

"I need to mark you because you're mine," he said as she heard him toe off his shoes, rip the shirt from his body, and then unbuckle his belt.

She thought he'd try to use his belt on her, but that was one thing she'd never stand for, and he knew it.

Nevertheless, she'd used that belt on him many times when he'd begged her to, when there was nothing else, and they were away from home the way they were now. But she thought he'd changed by the look in his eyes, and he wanted to punish her in ways he'd never done before.

Alex felt the bed dip, he sat on his thighs, and then leaned over her and pushed her hair to the side. It wasn't as loving as before where he gently reached and lay a swathe of her hair on the pillow after lowering his head to smell it, and then compliment her on how wonderful and fragrant it smelled.

She felt the warmth of his mouth as he leaned in, kissed her neck, his mouth easing down her back, each lick of his tongue bringing chills to her skin. "I want to see your face when you make love to me," Alex pleaded in a soft voice, her face filling the pillow.

"You will have plenty of time to see my face, but for now I don't want to see yours," Max said with the coolness of a stranger.

Alex should have resisted, moved away from him, done anything until he did as she asked, but she made that mistake, and before she could take a breath, his hands were between her legs, his arm resting under her stomach when he pulled her up on all fours, and as quick as that happened, he stroked his shaft and drove inside her opening when she wasn't ready for him.

A gasp and a moan filled the air.

Max didn't care. He wanted to fuck Alex hard, punish her, for what he didn't know, and at this time he didn't care. All he cared about was *not* making love to her, but fucking her hard and ruthlessly.

He'd always made love to Alex, even when they'd tied each other up. He'd spanked her, and she'd used a crop on him each time. It was love between the two of them. There was no one who could say it wasn't love, because no one but them existed in their room of pain, in their world of Max and Alex Blackstone.

It was their way of loving each other. Few would have understood it, but they did, however, now it was something entirely different, and Alex knew it.

She felt it as Max drove deeper inside her and never called out her name. All she heard were the groans of pleasure from his lips, and the smothered pain from hers.

Alex wanted to feel his body and she did—it was cold, not in temperature, but without feelings. She never thought this would happen to them. He fucked her body ruthlessly, not made love to her. She heard him moan as he pushed inside her and pulled out. She didn't feel his warm lips caress her back as before.

She felt him orgasm and never stop to ask if she wanted him to continue, but continue he did, until her body felt like a ragdoll as he pushed in and pulled out, fucking her for what appeared like hours in a position that was wearing her down, rotating from her opening, plunging into her anus, always with her on her stomach.

These were hard limits Max ignored with Alex.

Alex would let him finish abusing her in whatever fashion he chose, because she knew he'd been hurt by everything, and he'd been in an accident and maybe he wasn't himself. But when it was over she would lay down the rules, and afterwards she'd tell him how she felt about him and their sex life, and how it needed to be strengthened. Finally, she'd tell him she owed him a special kind of sexual punishment.

One he wouldn't enjoy.

Chapter 2

Alex woke with the sun flowing through the white shutters. She was sore as if her body had been invaded, and it had. At some point she'd just given in to Max, and let him have her the way he'd wanted with her lying there sore and unable to move.

Normally Max would have been lying with her exhausted, cuddling with her, complaining that he'd been bad, he deserved whatever punishment Alex deemed necessary, and she would eventually satisfy herself.

At home she'd order him to go to their room where she'd handcuff him, have her way with him because when he was restrained, his cock always hard, and she'd suck him off in seconds, and the next moment he'd be hard again, waiting for whatever punishment she could think of, because she'd tell him not to have an orgasm, and he would.

Only Alex had that kind of effect on Max. She alone could bring him to orgasm, and that was how it had always been since she'd met and fallen in love with him. It was her he needed to find peace, and to sleep at night. It was she who would bring him out of the darkness of his mind, give him strength, and renew his body for all the work he had to perform when running billion-dollar companies.

Well, he'd slept, however, now she wasn't sleeping in his arms as they had always done, and he wasn't in the bed beside her. Holding her.

Where the fuck was Max?

Alex shrugged her arms into one of the large shirts she'd found in the closet. Perhaps it belonged to Jonas. She didn't know, and she didn't care. It was time to talk to Max. It was time for her to tell him what happened last night, and now that he'd rested his mind by having sex, she felt he'd listen to her.

Barely walking, hobbling along she passed Jonas's bedroom, and when she glanced inside he was gone too.

She headed for the kitchen and she slowed down in front of the master bedroom, realizing what had happened in there last night. A chill crossed her body even as the door remained closed with yellow tape preventing anyone from entering. She hurried past it to go to the kitchen. As she entered the kitchen, she smelled coffee brewing, and saw Jonas sitting with his head down resting in his hands, and looking into his coffee cup.

"Are you okay, Jonas?" Of course, he wasn't okay. His wife he thought he'd be with the rest of his life had been killed by her lover in their bedroom while he slept next to her drunk. His wife's lover had committed suicide in their bedroom.

How the fuck could he be alright?

"I'm good," he admitted, his wide intense blue eyes turned up to greet Alex. "It's not the first time I've seen death." He reached for his cup with shaking hands, and had to hold it to his mouth with both palms.

Alex knew that Jonas wasn't good. How could he be? She wandered over to him, and she wrapped her arms around his chest and laid her head on his back, and he leaned his head into her breast and cried like a young boy.

"It will be alright, Jonas. Don't keep it in. I'm here for you. Max is here." It was then Jonas raised his head and passed his thumb under his eyes, and his eyes lit up.

"Where's Max? I thought he was dead. My God is it true, he's here?" There was life in his eyes now once he knew Max was there. "I thought it was a dream. I thought I heard him talking to you. So, it's not in my head."

"He was here last night. We slept in one of the bedrooms," Alex replied. Jonas hopped off the barstool and ran to the terrace and opened up the doors and peered out.

"Is he swimming? I don't see him," Jonas yelled, after leaning out through the opened door, then calling Max's name several times.

Alex stood alarmed, her heart beating so hard she thought it would burst through her chest. She rushed to the patio door standing beside Jonas. Then she pushed past him to stand on the outside for a better look. She placed her palm to her mouth.

Her eyes wandered across the sand and into the water, and nothing, only one early morning swimmer. Alex ran out, closer to the water to get a better look, and it wasn't Max. She would know him anywhere. She'd known that handsome face with thick dark hair, eyes deep blue like the ocean currents, shoulders wide and muscular, legs long and firm.

No, that man wading in the ocean water wasn't Max.

The man rising from the tide was an older man, as he rose, and Alex got a better look at him, her heart sank.

Alex's heart hammered in her chest as she rushed back to Jonas. "It's not him," she cried out. Then she hurried to find her phone. When she located it, she fumbled to swipe her thumb over it.

"Damn, what's taking it this long?" She read a message that she thought she'd never read again. Normally he'd never send her a text. He would have written a letter. He knew how she detested him leaving her notes and letters, but she didn't see why he had to text her. It seemed too impersonal that he would do such a thing. "Why didn't he wake me?" she voiced at a stunned Jonas.

Alex became afraid to read further? But she had to. She gathered her fears and strength and she realized that she would need all the strength she could muster to get through this text and through this day.

She inhaled and then exhaled and read the text.

Max: *Alex. I can't go on like this. I know none of this was your fault because it had to be Jonas, but you are his enabler the same way I was. He has managed to come between me and you, and my love for you is strained. I'm going home to take care of our children. Don't bother coming* *home. We should try to find other people that we can be happy with. You appeared to be happy with Jonas, and not me anymore. Stay with him. He needs you in ways I don't.*

Falling into the chair, Alex narrowed her eyes and furrowed her brow. Chills once again covered her body to the point that her hair prickled with pain. Anger and bitterness hadn't set in yet. She didn't think Max knew what he was saying. He was just acting out of jealousy and his own pain.

"What is it, Alex? What's happened to Max?" Jonas questioned, standing and looking over her shoulder and then turning her around to see her eyes.

Handing the phone off to Jonas, Alex stared into the house out through the glass doors, reaching the sand, and reaching into the ocean. She saw the tide move out and she didn't know what to do, and then she took a full breath in and exhaled once more.

"Why the fuck would Max say something so hurtful to you, Alex?" Jonas ranted after reading the text.

"Maybe he'd had enough of me and you," Alex said, bringing her attention back to Jonas. "He saw us lying in bed together and maybe he snapped. I'd never seen that darkness in his eyes, not for me. I'm not his blood. My children and you are. I'm perhaps someone disposable. I felt that way when I first met him. I was just an outlet to create the family he'd lost, keep you occupied, and take care of you while he left to handle business like the man he'd paid to watch me, and when that didn't work out he rid himself of him.

"You don't think he had Robert—"

"No. But he didn't prevent Robert from killing himself. I don't know what to think anymore, but I wouldn't bet on anything Max might do now. I don't really know Max. I would have been the last one to think that after all we've been through that he'd walk out on me and hurt me the way he has now. I know that he's vicious enough to take my children from me, because he tried it once before. I think he wants to break me, Jonas," Alex said, her voice pleading for an answer.

When she didn't get it from Jonas, she uttered, "If Max thinks I'll give up my children when I fought him to keep them, then he doesn't know me." Alex ambled over to the couch and sat. Then she glanced around and rose in a huff.

"Where are you going, Alex?"

"To bring Maximillian Blackstone to his knees." Alex meant that figuratively and literately. She had enough faith in herself that she knew if Max didn't mean what he'd said to her, he would regret the day he sent her that text.

Chapter 3

Jonas followed Alex into the bedroom. "What are you doing? Where are you going?" he questioned as she pulled her bag from the closet, and placed her few things into it. This was supposed to be a short visit, and Alex hadn't anticipated the drama that she'd found herself in. However, she should have known better.

Jonas was a walking drama. Wherever Jonas went, heartache, pain and tragedy followed, and there was Alex always in the middle of it. She didn't want this, she'd married into it. Shouldn't Max have known this and forgiven whatever had happened. Where was his understanding, for fuck's sake? Wasn't this his problem with himself, and his brother that he'd handed off to her?

She'd hoped that this would be different. How could it be different, because it was Jonas Blackstone after all, and when had her life been without drama after she'd met the two of them?

Alex couldn't remember.

Perhaps it was the time when she'd given birth and could get some rest being away from her wickedly handsome husband, Maximillian Blackstone, and his tragically handsome brother—Jonas?

Not even then did she get her peace when he'd insisted that he and his twin brother be inside the room when she gave birth. Max wanted Jonas to know that he was a part of his family, and nothing would destroy that bond. *Nothing but Max himself,* Alex thought.

After tossing into the suitcase the few clothes she'd brought with her, she turned to see Jonas leave. She had a black dress, a black pantsuit, white blouse, two pairs of black shoes, and a light-colored blue dress for the wedding, there was nothing else. Maybe if she'd packed her whip and crop, used it on Max she would have gotten a better response out of him.

It took that and more to get him to sleep when she first met him. That was where she'd made a mistake. If she'd done that he'd be sleeping by now, and she'd be cooking him breakfast, and telling him how much she loved him, and he'd be doing the same over coffee and breakfast.

When Jonas left after she was packing, he finally strolled back into the bedroom after she'd hurriedly showered and dressed, and was ready to leave.

Alex glanced into the mirror to see Jonas towering over her. With sad eyes, she made the announcement, "I'm leaving here, Jonas, and if you're smart you should leave too. Get out of Florida. The policemen said you weren't a suspect, but they suggested that you should get out of the area now, because they didn't want you here."

"But where are you going?" Jonas said, his voice low, tears pooling in his eyes like a lost child that'd been searching around for their mother and couldn't find her.

"Maybe home. I started out in New York and I'm going back. Maybe not Manhattan, but I'm going home."

After looking into Jonas's eyes and seeing how lost he was without Max, she decided it was only right that they stay together, if to do nothing else, but to give each other comfort.

Without Maximillian Blackstone they were lost. Well, one of them. Alex was sure that she'd be alright. She'd fought Max once for her son, and this time she wouldn't capitulate. She'd made up her mind she'd had enough. She hadn't chosen to be saddled with two outrageously dangerous men.

Dangerous in their own right. Max was dangerous because of his power and money. Jonas was dangerous because he was a loose cannon who attracted trouble, odd, sexy, beautiful women, like iron to a magnet.

Yet Alex felt responsible for Jonas in a sick possessive way. "You can come with me, and we can sort this out, or you can stay here, let your pain and memories catch up with you or the police, because sooner rather than later, they will be back, and asking questions about New York. In New York we can fade into the woodwork like so many people do.

"That's up to you because we don't have Max to depend on. We only have each other, and as much as I want to be rid of a Blackstone now, all I have is you, Jonas."

Alex placed her hands along his stubble jawline, and he closed his eyes and leaned into her palm.

"I know why Max left early and that was to get a head start to take my children and whatever else he planned. I really don't want to talk about it now. If you're coming, Jonas, pack a few things and leave the rest here for the next tenants to clean out. Don't leave any papers leading back to you."

⎯⎯⎯◉⎯⎯⎯

THEY WERE OUT OF JONAS'S rental in an hour, and waiting for a flight at the airport to New York. And then Alex realized that Jonas had a car. "What did you do with your car?"

"I told my friend that he could use it, but he had to get it out of the garage within an hour."

"How do you know he'll do that?"

"He just texted me and said he had it." Jonas sucked in a hard breath and walked on the plane with Alex. After relaxing in their seats, Jonas said, "What do we do now?"

"Get that car out of your name and into your friend's and give it to him. Get a hotel until we can lease an apartment."

"I mean what about Max? What are we going to do?"

"We're going to take Max on."

"Do you think that's a good idea, Alex?" Jonas questioned.

"Do you have a better one? Well, let's hear it. He accused you of falling in love with me, and that I was complicit in that too, and now he's out to take my children from me, what do you want me to do? I don't want to fight him, but he left me no choice. He thinks that he doesn't need me anymore, and he certainly doesn't need you. You did all his dirty work by posing as him for years, so he could grow an empire. I wouldn't be surprised if that cold-hearted bastard takes our money too."

"Do you think he'd do that? Max isn't like that," Jonas added, as if he'd been surprised at that statement by Alex.

"Yes. He'd do anything to dominate me and you. But I have money that he can't touch. It's my mother's inheritance, and if he were smart, which I know he is, he'd put a hold on the money I have in my bank account that he gave me when we were married. But I want to know just how far he'd go, that's why when I take him to court and ruin him, he won't have a penny left."

"You wouldn't do that, would you, Alex?"

Alex glanced over at Jonas and raised an eyebrow.

She was planning on much more than just taking his empire from him, she had other plans for Max because she knew his weakness, and she would exploit them to the fullest. What she had in mind would be hard limits.

When Alex lay back in her seat, she closed her eyes as Jonas glanced over at her. He'd never seen such a beautiful woman. When he'd first met her, she was naïve and young, and had never met men like him and his brother.

Just out of college and in love, Alex fought Max every inch to be with him, and for him to know that she was in love with only him, and she would never hurt him.

It was a tall task to bring him around, and for Max to ask her to marry him, but she did and then she made the mistake of trying to help his brother Jonas out, to save their marriage, and bring the peace they both craved, and that was when their marriage took a turn for the worse. Instead of creating a bond between Max, Alex, and Jonas, it tore them apart, with Max believing that Alex loved Jonas more than him.

That was what had triggered Max's anger—to think that his beautiful loving wife, Alexander Blackstone, desired another man over him, even if they were twins and Jonas was his devoted brother, and no one could tell them apart except maybe Alex.

In Max's mind that idea of deceit had been solidified, and he thought he knew the truth about his brother and Alex by the spectacle at Jonas's home on his wedding night. Instead of finding Jonas in bed with his wife, Max found Jonas in bed with *his* wife—Alex.

Jealousy overtook him and he couldn't see or understand anything that Alex had said. His only answer was to fuck her, take her hard, dominate her, and that's what he did. When he looked over at Alex sleeping naked, peacefully next to him, and he thought that another man, his brother had taken what belonged to him, Max stepped to the floor, took one last look at the woman who had controlled his mind and body, whom he'd loved above all others, he dressed, and in his mind he walked out of her life, and his brother's for good.

Chapter 4

Alex and Jonas arrived in Manhattan in the middle of a heat wave which wasn't unusual for what New Yorkers called a false spring. "Is that all you've brought with you, Jonas?" Alex said, her eyes taking stock of Jonas for the first time as she glanced down at his feet, and on them were flip-flops.

Jonas glanced down to see why Alex had furrowed her brow and aimed a disapproving glance his way. "They are expensive flip-flops, and this is an original hand-painted tee shirt," he uttered as they strode up to the security desk.

Jonas glanced over at her, "You said to leave some stuff, and I thought I could buy something later. Besides, I didn't have much in the way of clothing except for a few cargo shorts and tee shirts. Miami remember. The rest I left because of the memories. I'm trying to start anew in New York. No more bondage clubs and, well, you know. Do I have to spell it out?" Jonas whispered looking around to see if anyone had heard his conversation.

"My name is Mrs. Alexander Blackstone, and I called earlier and stated that I would be occupying my apartment for an indefinite time. I'd like to have my key now." Alex placed her identification in front of them. A passport and driver's license. One security guard reached and glanced at the papers.

"You can't use a Montana driver's license for identification in New York. You can drive a car here until you get your New York license, but I'm afraid that's all."

"Alex is here to pick up her keys to her apartment, not to get a lecture on the rules of the road," Jonas barked.

"And who are you?" One security guard who looked as though he'd never gone to a gym in his life, but spent his entire days ordering out for breakfast, dinner, and lunch, met Jonas's angry eyes. Jonas had been through too much to give a fuck any more.

"Never mind who I am, who the fuck are you to question Mrs. Blackstone? I demand that you give her the keys so we can get on with our lives."

The security guard who appeared to be playing the good cop turned to Alex, and said, "I'm sorry, Mrs. Blackstone, but the apartment was sold yesterday."

Alex's eyes quirked up. "By whom? Who sold my apartment?"

Good cop fumbled through the papers in front of him and looked up, meeting Alex's concerned eyes. "It seems your husband, Maximillian Blackstone, sold it to the new occupants. From what I heard from them, they had been trying to buy it and finally the deal came through." Alex turned and locked worried eyes with Jonas's.

It was Alex who told Max to sell everything, but he'd kept that apartment for her if she'd wanted to stay in Manhattan a few days for shopping trips, or as a place to get away from everything if she felt isolated in Montana. And today was that day, but she hadn't fathomed that it would be under these circumstances.

Alex turned in a daze forgetting about Jonas, who was still arguing with the security officer, and now his superior. When Alex reached the glass door and the doorman opened it, she realized that Jonas wasn't behind her, so she turned, and yelled, "Jonas, please. You're wasting your time and ours." In which case Jonas walked away, still turning to look back at the guards.

Standing outside with a backpack over his shoulder, and holding on to Alex's suitcase, Jonas stepped to the curb, raised his hand and a cab drove up. After Jonas opened the door, Alex slid into the back. When Jonas was inside, he said, "Take us to the Millennium Blackstone Hotel."

"No. Don't," Alex said leaning forward. "A Marriott."

"Which one?" the cabbie asked.

"I don't care as long as it isn't a Blackstone." When she settled back, Alex looked at Jonas, "Do you have any cash?"

"Not enough. I sank all my available funds into that bar and that car I had to give away. Max controls whatever money I have left, and I'm sure it would be a waste of time to expect him to place that into my bank account."

"What is he doing, Jonas?"

"Trying to punish us for being deceitful cheaters, something he's imagined. He will not stop until he destroys one or both of us."

"That will never happen." Alex crossed her arms in defiance. "I'm going to fight him. He's trying to take everything from me and you, and all of the love I had for him. I've been in love with him from the moment I laid eyes on his handsome face. And I've been honest with him, and he does this to me?" Alex murmured.

"It's who he is, Alex. He sees everyone including you and me as the enemy now. He will do whatever he can to bring both of us down even destroy us, because he thinks we love each other more than we love him."

"You and I know that's not true," Alex replied, wondering if there was something to that notion. She quickly dismissed it. It could have been true if she hadn't met and married Max. He had been all she'd ever wanted in life, and now for him to do this to her without a discussion between the three of them.

If Max didn't want to include Jonas in a family discussion, or a family therapy session, then he should have at least talked to her, but he said nothing and left the bed after ravaging her body all night while she voluntarily submitted to him.

Alex had been his Dom, and instead of her punishing him for his talk about her and Jonas, she submitted, because she thought that he needed a release. That had been a mistake.

"We know that there is nothing between us, but Max doesn't," Jonas added. Then Alex placed her palm over Jonas's as the cab came to a stop. Alex reached, opened her purse and pulled out her credit card. She swiped it and it came back as unauthorized, and after several tries the card still wouldn't go through.

"Lady you have to pay with cash, or I have to refer this to the cop over there, besides, I don't have all day," the cabbie barked.

"I have cash." Alex pulled out a twenty from her purse, and handed it to him." Alex rarely carried cash and she had only a couple of hundred dollars left. She had to get money or find the credit cards that Max had no access to, however, those were in her purse and safe at home, or the home she and Max had shared together.

Jonas stepped out of the cab in front of the hotel as she searched around for a credit card she thought Max hadn't known about. Finally, Alex found one. This was the very first card she had gotten in college, and thank god she used it on occasion and didn't cut it up after paying it off. "I have a card," she said to Jonas with a look of relief washing across her face.

Jonas had nothing to offer Alex at this time. He'd sunk all his money into a bar and buying the building, and his wife had said she needed extra money to send to her family. Jonas eagerly sent it to them without question.

After paying the cabbie, and checking into the hotel, Jonas and Alex were able to get a room. They stepped into the elevator with Jonas carrying their few things, got off on the top floor and stood in front of double doors.

When Jonas opened the door, he said, "You didn't have to get a suite. And one like this? We can't afford it," he gasped on opening the door.

It had been a long time since she heard that she couldn't afford something. It brought back painful memories of her past. Memories where she'd been homeless after her mother gave her up for adoption, and she didn't want to remain with a foster family. She'd run away as a teen, and by accident learned that her college had been paid for.

Alex didn't want to revisit those memories where she was struggling, unhappy, and worried about money all the time when she'd lived in Brooklyn. Money had been scarce when she tried to complete her education while buying food, paying rent, tuition, and trying to keep her grade point average up.

She had to do something and quick. When Jonas dropped his backpack and Alex's rolling suitcase in the foyer, he watched her as she walked into the large room and stood looking out of the floor to ceiling windows at the Manhattan skyline.

Turning around she spotted Jonas pacing on the terrace, and mumbling loudly to himself, "I've fucked up so much, and finally I've fucked you—" Alex cut him off. She placed her hand on his shoulder and then around his waist as she leaned her face on his back and placed a warm kiss. He craned his head to the side to see her. And that's when she saw such a hopeless look in Jonas's eyes.

Alex had seen that look before when a woman died in one of his clubs. She'd just witnessed it when his wife had her throat cut by her lover, leaving her lying beside him naked in a pool of her warm blood while he slept in a drunken state from too much celebration.

"No, you haven't," she added, when Jonas turned to face her. "You haven't fucked me... yet," she joked, and passed her hand across his five o'clock shadow. "Jonas, it's going to be alright. I have some money and we're going to be okay. Please, believe me. I'm going to call my lawyer, so get the bags and find our bedrooms, drop them in there, take a shave and shower, and by the time you get out, I'll have some money wired into my account."

Like a little boy following his mother's direction, Jonas smiled and did as Alex asked.

Alex sauntered to one of the large L sofas, sat, and pulled her phone out of her bag. "Gralen, this is Alex Blackstone."

"I recognized your voice, Mrs. Blackstone, how can I help you?"

"I'll need some money from my estate, and I need it ASAP. Can you get me something soon? Today."

"I understand the circumstances with your husband filing for divorce, and cutting you off from everything he owns, and taking a full page spread out in a major newspapers. Normally I'd say yes, but all your money is tied up. You'll have to forfeit your profits if you were to take it. As your business manager—"

Alex sat in disbelief. "I thought I heard you say that Max had filed for divorce, and he took out ads." Alex shuddered, doubting what she'd just heard from her business manager about Max. However, she'd expected something, but not this.

She didn't think that he would do something that heartless and cruel. She doubted that he would take her children, yet he'd attempted that with their firstborn. She thought that once Max got his head on straight and calmed down that he would know that she'd never been unfaithful to him with Jonas, or anyone. And yet, he'd had time to think, and still he carried out these mean and unscrupulous plans.

"Yes, Mrs. Blackstone. That's exactly what he did. Haven't you read the papers? What with the airplane accident maybe he isn't thinking as clearly as he should. I think you should talk to him." Alex's emotions filled what little space she had left to care about Max.

Alex knew there was no talking to Max, and he knew exactly what he was doing. Jonas had been right about him.

Max had gone on a mission to burn down, destroy, and abolish everything that they had together, and so far he'd succeeded, because now it would take a lot to keep Alex from fighting him where one wouldn't survive this, and she hoped after everything was over, that she would be standing, because she had children to raise who were waiting for their mother to come home and back to them.

What kind of heartless bastard had Maximillian Blackstone turned into? What kind of man would not respect the rights of a wife and a mother? She'd known all along, and she realized he'd been that kind of man before. He and Jonas had been raised by servants and strangers when their mother and father would leave them for years to go off on their trips around the world—his father on business trips and his mother to get away from the father where her excuse was that she'd go to Paris and Milan to shop.

Alex recalled Max telling her about the times alone with just him and Jonas, and he'd always taken care of Jonas because all they had were each other. Now he'd abandoned Jonas and her like his parents had done to them.

However, later their parents and extended family died in a plane crash, leaving only Jonas and Maximillian alone, with only a fortune to keep them company, and bring them unthinkable problems.

Chapter 5

After a quick shower, it was time to tell Jonas the truth. She sauntered into the living room to see Jonas listening to the news. "Do you believe this? Max had the balls to tell the world that he'd filed for divorce and he's not responsible for anything that you might buy."

Alex stood watching, and said, "At least he didn't say that he'd cut you off without a penny."

"That's because the money is not entirely all his. It's my inheritance and I worked for him, and he knows it. But what I think he has done is freeze everything, and used his lawyers to prevent me from getting to it. He thinks I want that money to be with you. To take care of you and to help get the children from him. He's right, and I bet I can't get any of it."

While Alex and Jonas slept and traveled to New York, Max had been busy.

"He probably made it so I can't access my money for a week or two, maybe a month or more."

"What are we going to do?" Jonas asked, as if Alex could solve all their problems, when in reality, she had been doing just that since she'd met him.

"As long as we don't check out of this place, we'll stay as long as they extend us credit. Jonas, we can only order from the hotel restaurant. I don't know when my attorney will be able to give me some of my money. I hope it's within a day, because what I have in my purse won't see us through a week with how expensive Manhattan is, and for Christ's sake don't drink anything from the mini bar."

"You're too late."

"I thought you'd stopped drinking." Alex closed her eyes and blew out a large breath.

"That was when I arrived in Florida, and before all this heavy shit just happened to me and you. I couldn't help myself, Alex. You understand. When you thought Max was dead you drank too. Why else did you fall asleep near me and didn't lock the doors?"

Jonas was right. Alex had drunk, and did fall asleep in his arms, but not because she was that drunk, because Jonas had been too strong for her to peel his arm from around her, and he'd acted as if he needed her to lie beside him, to give him comfort as he slept, like a baby who couldn't calm down without his blanket.

Alex paced through the room, and crossed her arms across her breasts looking out. She loved to see the Manhattan Skyline. It had been a dream of hers in Brooklyn living around the college. If she could only afford to live in Manhattan in a stylish and expensive apartment, and marry her dream man who could give her his love and a little money. She didn't need a lot of money, only a lot of love, then she'd be the happiest girl alive.

She'd finally gotten her wishes, but then like all things good and bad didn't last long. *Maybe misery lasts longer than happiness*, she thought.

Turning to see Jonas flicking through the channels of the large flat-screen television, she said, "Jonas. I'm going to call a friend of mine. Maybe she can get me a job in a hurry. We need money quick."

"If we need money, there's this lawyer who I dealt with before. He'd be glad to lend me some until I can convince Max that I'm entitled to what's mine, and—"

"Forget it, Jonas. I know the type of men you used to hang around with and who are your supposed friends, and I don't want to go down that road again with you. Try to do something to not get in trouble again. We can't afford to let Max get any more dirt on us than he already has. My friend has a modeling agency, but I think I'm not too old to get something, however, they're looking for women in their twenties for commercials. Something that will pay for our food until next week or a month if we're unlucky."

"But, Alex—" Jonas pleaded, before Alex interrupted him.

"Look, Jonas. I've been around you too long. I love that you want to contribute, but we can't afford for you to go to one of your friends and get in more trouble. We've been out of Manhattan for only two years. That's not long enough for people to forget your club, and what happened there."

"But this man who's willing to lend me money doesn't want anything from me. He just wants a friend. I did him a few favors, and he said that if I needed anything he'd gladly return the gesture." Alex shuddered to think what favors Jonas could have done operating his infamous bondage club.

"I'm terrified to ask what kind of favors you did for him."

"Tie him up and have some woman just whip his ass. That's all. Nothing heavy."

"I knew it, Jonas."

"But you don't understand, Alex. He wasn't like all the other men, not even like Max or me. This man is a younger man than Max and me. He'd gotten into an accident on his way to enlist into the army, unlike me, he didn't make it to his post, and, unlike me, his injuries were physical. My injuries were more of the mind, but his were physical. Not his face, not his legs, but only his groin."

Alex turned and sat down near Jonas, because she'd been interested in what had happened to this young men who'd incurred all kinds of injuries, and especially if he was young. She'd seen some veterans without limbs. It must have been difficult for them, but she didn't know how much pain they had endured because of their injuries at such a young age. She'd known what Jonas had gone through, because of his injuries to his mind, and the results which were drinking and drugs.

She'd bet Jonas's friend had suffered both mentally and physically. She couldn't imagine what he'd gone through.

Jonas explained how the young man had been born into money, and because he wanted to prove to his father that he wasn't a selfish entitled son of a bitch, he did something stupid. He took his privileged life, placed it on the line when he joined the marines, but he didn't quite make it. He had an accident in his sports car.

"Like you did with your life," Alex interjected.

"Like me." And Jonas continued telling Alex what the young man had done, and what it had cost him—his manhood. When he'd gotten out of the hospital and had a chance to heal his body, he visited his club hoping to get some fulfillment in his life if just for a moment.

"There wasn't anything left for him. His girlfriends wanted no part of a cripple," Jonas said, as if he'd mirrored the same life as this young man.

"But he wasn't cripple—" Alex questioned, and Jonas interrupted.

"He was a young man of twenty-five without a penis. Need I say more? He couldn't have children, and he couldn't have sex. He wanted it, but he couldn't do anything. With his money the doctors managed to put his body back together, but not his mind. He could have an orgasm, it was difficult, but not impossible."

Alex sat and listened to the tragic story, and she felt sorry for him. "Why don't you come with me to see him, Alex? He's a nice guy to be around, and you don't have to let him know that I told you about his troubles. He loves to look at beautiful women, and once I tell him what you're trying to do to get your children back, I know he'd give me or you the money."

"I don't want him to give me or you anything. I would consider it a loan for a month no more," she warned.

"That sounds like you've given up the idea about doing a commercial to get who knows what, and you'll probably have to get in the union, and that will cost a pretty penny, and after all your work we still won't have enough to make it through the month. The longer it takes to get money together, the better it is for Max to do us more harm."

Alex thought about what Jonas said, and she had to choose the lesser of two evils, and she hoped she would make the best choice.

"Since you put it like that, then I'll go with you, Jonas. Call him and tell him we'll visit him tomorrow. I need some food and rest today," Alex said. "And, Jonas, don't offer him something that you can't deliver."

Jonas rose from the sofa with a smile and headed to where he'd placed his phone. Then he turned, stopped, and glanced at Alex. "You're doing the right thing for us."

Did Jonas say "for us", Alex thought?

There is no *us* and there will never be. Alex's only thought was to get Max back by any means necessary. She wanted her family, and if Jonas had any sense he'd spend his time trying to get a life that was worth something. Get a woman that would understand him and have a family. Alex wasn't on the market, at least she didn't think of herself as that, whether Max thought of her that way that was his problem to solve, because she thought of herself as Mrs. Blackstone, and she wasn't about to relinquished that title—not for Max or anyone.

Chapter 6

The next day Jonas assured Alex that his friend would see them, and he especially wanted to see her up close. The woman who called herself Alex Blackstone who had captured the heart of the most sought-after bachelor in the world.

He'd heard her name and seen her in the papers with her husband, Maximillian Blackstone, who had been his idol. When he saw the woman called Alex on Max's arm, he wanted a woman who looked just like her, because to him she was the most beautiful woman in the world with her seductive brown eyes and dark flowing hair.

Jonas's friend thought Alex was stunning in her photos and on television, and he wondered if the pictures did her justice. And he had a need to see whether she was as beautiful and drop-dead gorgeous in person as she'd appeared in magazines, and to him.

Jonas didn't tell Alex that his friend had requested her services when he owned his infamous BDSM club. He had to disappoint him, because at the time she serviced only one man, and that was Max, her husband, but then neither Max nor Christian Kenley knew that she'd worked for Jonas as a favor to him.

At the time, Max didn't realize that his own wife had been the mysterious bondage Dominatrix. Maybe it was that which had Max filled with simmering resentment toward Jonas. Even Christian Kenley couldn't understand why Jonas wouldn't share his mysterious Dominatrix with him when he needed her services after his accident.

Alex and Jonas took the first cab that pulled up to the hotel entrance and climbed in. "Fifth Avenue," Jonas had said to the cabbie.

"You didn't say he lived on Fifth Avenue. What is his name anyway? I can't call him friend, or friend of Jonas."

"His name is Christian Kenley."

"Do you mean to say he's the heir to the Kenley Oil fortune?"

"Yes, and much more."

"He's an only child. That means he will never—"

"Never be able to have children," Alex interrupted grimly as she gazed out the car window watching the crowds of people walking along the street window shopping, rushing around to pick up lunch, and heading back to work maybe after an extended lunch hour.

Alex missed working, but she thought she had the most important job there was, and that was to raise her children. But now Max had stolen that from her along with everything else in her life that she loved.

She'd made up her mind, she'd vowed that after the last horrible thing that had happened to her when she'd been separated from herself, her husband, and children, that she would never leave them again.

Jonas's wedding would be a simple thing, she'd thought. She'd help Jonas and show support for him and prove that he had a family that cared about him.

That would have been one day. Only one day, and she'd fly back to her family and with her husband, and let someone else take care of Jonas. But it wasn't that simple. Nothing with Jonas Blackstone was ever that simple.

As they neared their destination, Alex turned to Jonas, "I had tried to get an apartment in that building for years," Alex commented in a low voice once the cabbie slowed in front of the building on Fifth Avenue in the heart of the most expensive real-estate in the world.

When the car came to a stop, and Jonas had paid with Alex's card, he reached into his pocket and dropped his last twenty dollars as a tip, Alex chastised him. "You shouldn't have done that. That may be the last money we have."

Standing on the sidewalk in the middle of crowds walking around them, Jonas took Alex's hand, and said, "Don't worry. I have this covered." Alex didn't want to tell Jonas just what she thought about his statement. She'd heard it before, and all he had covered was a dead body that she'd help him hide.

No wonder Max couldn't take any more, but Jonas was his problem, and when did it become mine? she thought as they stood at the elevator when security asked them questions and asked to see identification. After showing their IDs, he opened the elevator and sent them up to the penthouse.

When the door opened, Christian Kenley stood in a magnificent dark-blue suit with a white shirt, without a tie, and on that shirt gold cufflinks. She remembered how elegant Max had been when she first met him, and even lately after his plane crashed. Alex didn't think that anyone would be that handsome with his suit covered with dirt. That was until she looked into the green eyes of Christian Kenley.

"Alex, this is Christian, and Christian this is my sister-in-law Alexander Blackstone."

"Is that spelled with a *re* or *er*?" Christian's smile raced across his face and lit up his green eyes. He showed an unusual amount of attention to Alex. *What the fuck does it matter how her name is spelled,* Jonas thought.

Then he looked over to Alex, and she appeared to be mesmerized by Christian. Her smile was equally broad.

Christian was an extremely handsome young man in his early twenties, six feet one, and a well-toned body. *A great package, but nothing inside,* Jonas thought.

Jonas glanced between Alex and Christian, and Christian held out his hand, and Alex placed her palm inside his and they gazed at each other. Clearly there was some kind of connection, and Jonas didn't like it. But what kind of connection could Alex have with a man like Christian. Of course he was good-looking, single and rich, but he had this handicap. He couldn't have sex with Alex, well, not in the traditional sense.

Jonas passed his hand over the two hands belonging to Christian and Alex, and somehow that spell was broken, and they both turned and smiled at Jonas.

"Jonas and Alex, please come in. We have a lot to discuss," Christian said as he walked between Jonas and Alex after raising his arm, and Alex tucked hers under his, and he placed a warm palm over her hand.

They strolled into the vast living area, where Christian seated Alex on a velvet sofa where she could look out and experience the glorious view. "I've never seen anything like this," Alex said with a closed smile aimed at Christian.

"I'm sure you have. You are Alex Blackstone after all."

"But there are views and there are *views*," Alex said, offering Christian a wide full-toothed smile.

Christian stared and offered her a wide grin. Everyone had always complimented him on his beautiful smile after they'd lauded how handsome a man he was once he'd turned twenty-five.

Jonas opted to sit across from Christian and Alex. He wanted to watch the two. Not that he thought Alex would be interested in Christian. How could she? She had his brother and him, of course.

Or did she?

Jonas knew that she'd always have him by her side if she needed anything, but now with Max acting like a dick, Jonas wasn't sure about anything anymore.

"Yes, the view from where I'm sitting is stunning," Christian complimented, and Jonas realized that Christian wasn't looking out, but his view was dead-centered on Alex. "Would you like something to eat, or something to drink? I asked my cooks to prepare a spectacular dish for the both of you. Whatever you desire, I'll have them cook it for you now."

Christian pressed a silent buzzer, and his chef, a large woman, came in and presented them with menus and then she left. "Just take your time and decide. Would you like a drink? Wine maybe?"

"I'll have a glass of wine," Alex said.

"I don't drink anymore," Jonas declared. Alex glanced across at him. "We came to discuss business not have lunch—"

"Maybe Alex would like to stay and have dinner with me, and you can go back to the hotel or wherever you'd like. I can have my driver take you back."

Alex watched Jonas, and knew he was getting agitated by the way Christian became instantly enamored with her, and she didn't want him to say or do something rash and screw up her chances of borrowing money to keep them going until she could get her money.

They needed the money like yesterday. Never had she thought she'd be in a position like this ever again. She thought that having money would prevent her from needing it. She had all the money she'd desired to keep her comfortable, but she didn't have the money now when she really needed it. There would be a lag between the time she got the money, and she needed it to live, and she couldn't allow Jonas to fuck that up by getting jealous, or being overly protective of his brother who had cast them into this chaos of uncertainty.

"We can all have dinner together, but first we should discuss why we're here—" Christian interrupted Alex, and turned to her.

"I know why you're here and before you say anything you can borrow as much money as you need. There are no stipulations on the money, except maybe have dinner with me—alone." When he said *alone* he turned to Jonas. "Jonas must have told you that I'm harmless."

Alex's eyes fell to the floor in embarrassment. He'd known Jonas before, and naturally he'd known how he behaved, and how any man around Alex must have wanted her, even if he didn't have the equipment to have her.

Nevertheless, Jonas had all the equipment now that his stupid brother, Max, had put Alex in a tenuous situation.

"I will sign the contract," Alex said, "If you have your lawyers draw it up and I can get the money by tomorrow. I would be very appreciative of that." Her eyes met Christian's soft eyes. Christian raised a thick eyebrow and turned to Alex with his piercing green eyes and aimed a pampered smile her way.

"You can have the money now at this moment. I don't want to have you sign a contract or anything else. I'm giving you this as a loan, but I wanted to make this a present to you, however, I knew that you wouldn't accept it. Maybe next time I can give you something you don't want to give back."

Jonas watched in shock and apprehension. He knew where Christian was going with that, and he had to intervene.

"Alex and I are in need of the money until our funds come due. We're planning to open a business," Jonas said with a shaky voice. Jonas's voice wobbled a bit whenever he lied.

Christian laughed because he knew the whole story. "I have no interest in what you want the money for, only that Alex needs it. Don't think I'm a fool, Jonas. I know what your brother has done to you, and this beautiful woman, and he's the fool. I just want her to have a chance to fight him for her children and anything else she wants to do to him. It's all in the papers and on CNN. He really is hurt, but from what I read he has no right to be. What man would throw the baby and the bathwater out, but an arrogant man who must have found someone else to satisfy his lust."

Alex furrowed her brow and narrowed her glance at Christian. His words were piercing and unsettling.

"I know a little about Maximillian Blackstone and before this day, I'd envied him. He had a reputation around New York. I think I was privy to his antics at your club, Jonas."

Jonas had been in deep thought and Christian might have caught him thinking about what he'd done by bringing Alex here to talk to Christian Kenley. Clearly it was a mistake, but Jonas couldn't do anything now. He couldn't un-fuck this decision. Then he turned his attention to Christian.

Alex looked on and in silence, and wondered if that could be true what Christian was suggesting. Now that Christian had sown doubt into her relationship with Max, it hurt. Never had she thought anything could upset her that much. Jonas's knowing glance turned to Alex from watching Christian. Alex had been trying to maintain a good front, pretending to be cool and unaffected by Max's behavior toward her, but Jonas knew her every expression, and the way she clasped her hands, to the way she changed her position when she sat. Those mannerisms signaled that she was upset.

"My brother is not a fool. He's just disappointed and he'd recently been in a plane crash, and he isn't thinking clearly. When he comes to his senses, he'll realize that he's made a mistake and will come to Alex on his knees begging."

"When will that be?" Christian said dryly and crossed his arms and turned slightly to Alex. "Did you know he filed for a divorce, and had gotten a judge to grant it?" Christian locked eyes with Alex, who appeared to be in shock.

Jonas reached for the Daily News, sitting alongside the New York's Times, picked up the morning paper and read the headlines.

Maximillian Blackstone the Rich Industrialist files for a Divorce from his beautiful wife, and is granted one in a day. Go figure.

When could Max have had the time to get a judge to sign off on that? Jonas wondered. Then he looked at the name of the judge who'd signed that obviously illegal paper.

Jonas knew that name—Caulfield. For the right price, Judge Caulfield would sign anything. Caulfield had been Max's go-to judge when he needed to get Jonas out of jail for marrying an underage girl in Las Vegas. Caulfield had offered his signature for a price on just about anything that Max had to clean up for Jonas to get him out of a million fucked-up situations.

Jonas knew Alex was in trouble.

Chapter 7

When Christian's driver drove Jonas and Alex home, silence filled the car, filled the space between Jonas and Alex, filled the hotel suite that they had to live in together until they could go their separate ways, but that would be much longer than they had anticipated.

Max had thrown down the gauntlet, got in the first blow that almost took Alex's breath away. She didn't expect him to get his divorce, file for it, *yes,* but have it finalized without her, and she didn't have a chance to fight it. No, all that came as a shock.

Jonas had warned her about what Max was capable of doing but she wouldn't listen to him. Alex thought she knew him better, but now her heart was broken, and she didn't think he was capable of breaking it more, and then this.

Not only did he take her children, her livelihood, and tried to kill what love she had left for him, but he had almost destroyed her.

Alex opened the hotel door, sat down, and tried to make sense of everything, then she looked at Jonas. "Why didn't you tell me that he was ruthless and heartless?"

"I told you, but you didn't want to hear me. Just like I'm telling you now don't get involved with Christian."

"But you brought me to him." Alex sat back and closed her eyes, and toed off her shoes. Jonas rushed to Alex's side and sat on the floor and massaged her feet. "No don't do that," she said, looking down at him. "Sit beside me." Alex patted the cushion beside her.

When Jonas sat, he looked at Alex, and issued another warning, "Yes, I know I was foolish enough to ask you to come with me, but I'm warning you again, don't get involved with him, and pay him back as soon as you can," Jonas advised.

"I'd planned on doing just that, but first I have to teach Max a lesson he will never forget. If you try to hurt someone you love by being hard and callous, then you'd better know what you're doing." Alex's eyes grew dark. She stared out past the view of Manhattan and buildings, as if to reach out and snatch Max's heart out of his body—if he had a heart.

"What are you planning, Alex? I see your beautiful face and the mischief in your eyes, and I know something is coming, and it's not going to be pretty."

"I want to see my children first. Does Christian have a jet?"

"Of course."

"I'm going to ask him to use it to go to our Montana home, and I'm going to take my children while Max is away looking after all his shit. With the money that I get from my inheritance, and borrow from Christian, I can keep Max in court and away from me, until I can make him realize how much I love him, and how much he loves me. I've never needed anyone in my life as much as I've needed Max. Maximillian is the only man I'll ever want, and I'll be damned if I let him go that easily—especially after what he's done to me."

Jonas brought Alex into his arms, and he thought he saw tears pooling in her eyes and he brought her closer. "I just wanted to help you, Jonas. It was all for Max. I could have stayed and cared for my children, but you were like one of my children."

Alex glanced at Jonas with her teary brown eyes, "You were like a wayward child, Jonas. You know they have one in every family. I thought if I could help out with you, then it would lighten the burden on Max, and it did, but it brought on other thoughtless consequences. He thinks I love you in a sexual way."

Jonas didn't respond, because he knew his heart, but he knew Alex never felt about him the way she felt about Max. She never would, even if Max wasn't in the picture, she'd never love him that way. The way he'd envisioned. To have her in his arms, to be able to see her beautiful body when she'd become pregnant for him.

That was just a fantasy he'd likely keep to himself.

Jonas stood as Alex held on to his hand. "I have to take a shower, and I have things to do. I can't let you take care of me. I have to find a way to get my money from Max." Jonas let Alex's hand slip from his, and he wandered into his room, sat on the bed, and made a call to Max. He didn't answer after several rings, so Jonas decided to text him and use the strongest words possible. Max responded to his texts, but Jonas needed to hear Max's voice.

Jonas: Max, what the fuck are you doing?

Max: I'm busy, call me back later.

Jonas: I deserve an answer, and Alex does too.

Max: Why should I talk to someone who's been fucking my wife?

Jonas: Are you that delusional and your thinking is so morbid that you would think that I, or better yet, Alex, would do something like that you. Have you had your head checked out, because I think you've lost your mind in that plane accident?

No text came in and then the phone rang. It was Max. "What the fuck are you calling me and texting me for, Jonas. And how dare you suggest that I could be wrong about you and Alex?"

"Well, who the fuck are you that you think that no one is to question your thinking. I called to ask about my money. I need you to place some in my account so I can help Alex. You took everything from her. Her children—"

Max's voice lowered to a disturbing level. "They're my children too. I have a fucking right to them since Alex found it necessary to leave them with nannies to go off with you and your fucked-up life."

"She didn't go off with me. You are the one who doesn't deserve the children and Alex."

"Now we're getting to the heart of the matter. You want that money to take care of Alex. Do you think I would release money so you can go off with my wife?"

"I thought you didn't want her. You got a divorce for fuck's sake. You've taken everything from her. What more do you want?" Jonas asked, and he added, "She's no longer your fucking wife."

Max's silence and anger could be felt through the phone as Jonas waited for a response.

"I want her to come to me. I'm her Master, her Dominant, and she treated me as if you are. I need to know that I'm in control."

"You've always been in control, Max. She adores you. She'd do anything for you, but you're the one who's running her away into another man's arms."

There was silence, and then Max added, "Is she running into your arms?"

"For Christ's sake, Max, have you completely lost your mind? Did you hear anything I've had to say? She's enlisted Christian Kenley to help her."

"I have to go. I'll get back to you." Max hit the red button on his phone, and Jonas sat on his bed breathless. He knew he couldn't tell Max that he was the one to get Alex involved with Christian Kenley. That alone would seal his fate with his brother.

Chapter 8

Alex woke, ordered a light breakfast for herself—fruit, a toasted bagel, yogurt, and coffee. Jonas preferred something heavy, a steak and eggs. Then she sat up in bed and gazed around her room. Never had she felt so alone as now. However, she wasn't alone because sleeping in the next room was Jonas Blackstone.

When Jonas sauntered into the living area, Alex was headed to Jonas's bedroom to tell him breakfast had been delivered. She'd known what he wanted for breakfast, because he ate one meal a day, and rarely had he eaten past six in the evening.

However, Alex needed her coffee, fruit, yogurt and lunch to keep her going. Jonas kissed Alex on the forehead before he sat across from her, "How are you feeling today?"

"Better. But I miss my children. I tried calling them and they didn't answer."

"They're in school at this time," Jonas added, reaching for the coffee pot before throwing the complimentary morning paper across the room. He didn't want any bad news this early because he'd been set on enjoying his morning.

"You're probably right, Jonas."

Jonas glanced over at Alex. "Where are you going?" He noticed that she had worn a dress to eat. A revealing one, too. Off her shoulders, showing off her smooth, tanned skin from a few days in Florida. Her legs were as gorgeous as he remembered, now that they didn't have pants to hide how lovely they were.

Jonas had seen Alex in pants most times, and she would occasionally wear shorts when the weather had been suitable in Montana. Very seldom did he get a good look at her in a dress until now, and she was stunning in a yellow dress. "Why don't you let me take you to lunch or dinner later?" Jonas questioned, and waited for an answer.

Alex rose from her seat after drinking a cup of coffee, turned, and paced to the window to peer out. "I have to get some money from the bank Christian wired into my account yesterday."

She paused, wondering if she should tell Jonas her plans. She thought it best to reveal to Jonas her plans for today, because she knew he wouldn't stop asking to take her to dinner.

They had only each other now and Jonas needed something to do. Alex couldn't wait until Max made another move. How did she know Max wasn't capable of getting to Christian if he found out that Christian had given her a loan? Max had all kinds of connections and that was what Alex was afraid of.

"I'm having lunch with Christian." She waited for him to respond, and respond he did.

Jonas dropped his fork and knife onto the plate, with it making a clattering sound, where she turned and strolled in Jonas's direction and stood at the table. He looked up at Alex. "You're doing what?" he barked.

"You heard me, Jonas."

"But you can't. You're a married woman."

"That's over and you know it," Alex admitted with conviction. She'd finally accepted the inevitable. Now it was time for Jonas to accept it too. *Max didn't waste any time getting rid of me, and why should I waste my time thinking and moaning over him?* she thought.

Jonas stood and his breathing became shallow. It was all his fault. He knew he shouldn't have pulled Alex into another one of his troubles waiting to happen, because if Max had found out that she'd met Christian through him, that would be it. Max would totally disown him.

"Alex, you can't get involved with Christian other than with this business arrangement. You don't know this man. He's too powerful and... Max would never forgive us."

"I don't give a damn what Max feels or wants. He should have thought about me and you before he started trying to destroy me. What does he want from me? I've given him everything and he does this to me."

Alex marched around the suite searching for her phone and purse, with Jonas following after her. "We just have to give it some time. Max will come to his senses. He loves you, Alex. He just wants... you to himself. He said—"

"You fucking talked to him? Don't you know that's what he wants you to do? He wants his way with everything. The selfish dominating prick. He got my children, got me to help you, and then became angry after I saved him the trouble of dealing with your problems so he could carry on with his business. He loves his fucking companies more than he ever loved me, or you and perhaps the children too. If he loves me... then he will have to work for my love."

Alex felt that Max hadn't work hard enough to keep her, and if he wanted her now she wouldn't make it easy for him.

Alex picked up a book and newspapers on the table. "Here is my damn phone and purse." Alex tucked her phone into her purse and headed for the door. "I'll meet you for dinner at this steak house off Fifth Avenue. You know the one. It's right around the corner from your defunct club. Be there at eight and wear a tie. Get a suit and charge it to me. Buy some suits, ties, shirts, and shoes the kind Max would wear."

Jonas wondered why he had to buy clothes like Max, and then it came to him why she'd requested that he do this.

"That's expensive, Alex."

"Why are you worried? You're not paying for it, and if it was up to your brother you would be sleeping on the street. Can't you see what he has done, Jonas? The only people who loved him unconditionally, he has tried to hurt and destroy. Why should I love him more than I love myself, and why should you keep faith with him when he doesn't keep faith with you?"

Alex opened the door, turned, and gazed in Jonas's direction.

Alex had given Jonas a lot to think about, and yet he couldn't bring himself to feel anything but love for Max. *Max has sacrificed his life to take care of me,* Jonas thought. *Even if he enlisted a surrogate to do that.*

Jonas loved the way Alex had filled the void when he needed a friend and needed his brother.

Standing at the door watching Alex leave and get into the elevator and disappear, Jonas headed for the shower. He wondered why Alex wanted him to buy expensive suits, but then he knew, but he didn't know what the undertaking would be. He just knew that when it was over, someone would be injured, and he hoped it wouldn't be him because he couldn't take too much more. He'd been on the edge since his wife died, and too busy to think about it, and he'd been thankful for that.

———⊙———

WHEN ALEX STEPPED OUTSIDE the hotel, a limo was driving up. The driver exited the black SUV, strode up and opened the door. She had seen him on the last trip to the hotel and he'd been pleasant, polite and professional. "Where would you like to go, Mrs. Blackstone?"

"To the nearest Chase Bank." The driver a man in his early sixties with grey hair, penetrating knowing eyes, wearing a dark suit nodded his head, and entered the driver's side, started the car, angled it into the busy traffic.

After driving a short distance to Madison Avenue to the main bank a large structure that appeared to take up most of the block, the limo came to a stop, and Alex waited for him to open the door.

She didn't want him opening doors for her each time, because lately she'd been doing things like that herself. She'd driven her children to school, bought and carried her own groceries, and gone to PTA meetings like everyone else. She wasn't special and she didn't want to be treated like a pampered housewife with too much money and time. She just wanted to be Maximillian Blackstone's wife, but that carried its own select advantages as well as a set of misfortunes and problems.

When the door opened Alex stepped out and onto the sidewalk, and sauntered into the bank.

After opening another account and transferring the money Christian had placed into her account, she strolled out feeling more relaxed than she had been since all this agonizing problems with Max and Jonas began.

Climbing back into the SUV, she requested to be taken to Christian's apartment.

Looking down at her watch, she knew it was time for lunch, and she would have to meet with Christian if only to show her gratitude. But damn he was handsome with those green eyes, and that muscular body which belied the fact that he'd been in a car accident, and he no longer had parts of his body that would have probably attracted her to him otherwise.

She let out a sigh. "Ah too bad." *He would have made a perfect fake boyfriend,* she thought.

It was a cruel twist of nature that a man as stunning in looks as Christian who didn't have a scratch on his handsome face, not a scar on his body that Alex could see, except the fact that he couldn't have sex, and would never have children unless he adopted. Since he wasn't engaged, or had a regular girlfriend that Alex knew of, she thought that his future would be unhappy and unclear.

Alex sucked in a breath standing before Christian's door when it opened, and a woman stood glaring at her. She appeared to be in her early fifties and of Spanish descent. She smiled and addressed Alex in

Spanish where Alex answered her. She said to Alex that she had been Christian's maid for a number of years, and before that her mother had worked for Christian's father and mother before they passed away.

The maid ushered Alex into the same exquisite room that she'd met him in the day before. When she glanced up, he stood in the sunlight, and she thought how handsome a man he was. She remembered seeing Max who had been older at the time, and she thought there was no man who could compare to him in looks, and then she met Jonas.

And now Christian Kenley.

However, Christian was a different kind of man. A man who'd suffered not in the ways Jonas had, but in a profound deep way, and although Alex was attracted to him, she felt sorry for him. She knew he had to be proud, and she'd never say anything unless Christian revealed his situation to her first. But then he had to know Jonas, and figured Jonas had told her.

"You are indeed every bit as beautiful as your pictures. I think I said that yesterday and if for some reason I was stupid enough not to compliment you on your beauty, please forgive me." He sauntered over to her with his drop-dead gorgeous smile, and his wide shoulders, and long legs closing the distance between them.

Christian reached for her hand, went to his knees in front of her, and his warm mouth caressed the palm and top of her hand which startled Alex. He gazed up at her and his eyes bored through to her core. *What is happening to me?* she thought. *No man has affected me, but Max. Maximillian where are you? Why are you leaving me to flounder, and have a man seduce me this way?* Under any other circumstances she would have repelled Christian's advances, but she knew that they could never have any kind of relationship the way a man and woman would, therefore, she offered him a warm attentive smile.

And then Christian said the unthinkable.

"Would you marry me now that you're a newly divorced woman? Just say the word and we could be on a plane to Las Vegas. I can get everything arranged with my lawyer, and in a few days you can be Mrs. Kenley."

Alex sat back stunned. Her eyes wide as her open mouth, and she looked down at this twenty-something handsome-looking man, and said, "I'm older than you, surely you can find a woman your age, and I have children."

"I don't care, and what are you, two years older than me? That's nothing. Your children can be mine as well. I want children."

"Why don't you have them?" She didn't mean to say that, and she wished she hadn't because she saw the painful look on Christian's face.

Christian stood and sat beside her. "I think it's time to address the elephant in the room. It's been there since you walked into my home, and I knew, and you knew about me."

"Then, how could you ask me to marry you?" Alex questioned.

"Because, I've wanted a woman like you all my life, and I see my opportunity to have you. If you discover that you still love your husband and you want to return to him, then I won't stand in your way. I'll put that into our contract."

"Is that all I am, an opportunity, a contract?"

"You are much more, and if you allow me, I'll show you how much more you are to me, and I can be to you. I know you're attracted to me, and I'd be a fool not be attracted to a desirable woman like yourself. If you give me half a chance you wouldn't miss that I can't have sex with you the ordinary way, but together we can find a way where we both can be satisfied. I know all about you. You have been Maximillian Blackstone's Dominatrix."

"Where did you find that out?"

"I have ways. I'm a man with money, and I don't mind spending it to get and find out the things I need to."

Alex pulled away. "You're moving too fast for me. I can't think, and I'm still in love with my husband. I can't emphasize that enough. I can't open my heart to you this soon. I don't have any room for anyone but Max."

"I'm willing to give you as much time as you need. What else do I have to do besides chase the most beautiful woman I'd ever laid eyes on?"

It was at this time Alex had lost her appetite and her way. She had been flattered, excited, and terrified all at the same time. She had to get away from this young man. He'd scared her with his proposal. He'd been closer to her age than Max. Max was eight years her senior and Max had been her Dominant, and she'd been his Mistress in the bed. Never on the outside.

Alex and Max had come to an agreement that they'd switch roles when it was needed.

Max had called the shots. He'd decided when he should sell off his vast business empire and she knew it. When she'd asked him to be home with her more and get rid of some of his hotels, he'd placated her and told her he would, but he never did. He'd allowed her to think that she controlled something.

The only thing she'd controlled was him in bed, and now she'd lost that as well.

Alex finally discovered that she didn't run anything, not even him. She'd only been a disposable product like everything else he'd owned.

"I have to go. I have something very important to take care of," Alex admitted.

"You haven't eaten," he said. She rose with Christian holding on to her hand.

"I really should go," Alex insisted, looking down at his hand clutching hers tightly.

"You will be back, won't you? I hope it's not anything I said, or maybe I came on a little too strong?"

"No. No. It wasn't that." *But of course, it was that,* Alex thought. She'd been bewildered and getting more confused since she'd been in

Christian's presence. He was all the things she'd dreamed about years before meeting Max.

She'd thought she'd wanted a man his age.

Handsome, rich, young, tall, warm, and smart. However, he was a few years too late. Where was he when she'd been suffering in Brooklyn, and could barely feed herself after college? Where was he when she'd found Max and became pregnant by him, and he didn't realize that she had his baby? Where was Christian when Max had threatened to take away her son and had done so? She should have run from Max then, but she loved him, and she stayed.

Now here came Christian who wanted to marry her, and she was torn and still in the same position as she had been in when she'd gotten pregnant by Max, and when he wanted to take her son and now he wanted all her children, for what? To control her further.

The controlling bastard, Alex thought, as she climbed into the limo and called Jonas.

Chapter 9

"Jonas, meet me in twenty minutes at the Millennium Hotel," Alex exclaimed as Christian's limo headed uptown to Fifth Avenue. I need to purchase something. Wear your best suit. You did get a suit?"

"Yeah, but they're sending it tomorrow. I thought you were having lunch with Christian."

"We don't need to talk about that now. I have something to tell you, and I need your advice."

"When it comes to Christian, the only advice I can give you is stay away, and beware."

"You didn't say that yesterday. You led me to believe he was a tragic figure who had given up on life, and now I discover that he not only hasn't given up on life, but he—look Jonas the car is stopping and I have to hurry. Remember in twenty minutes meet me at—"

"Max's hotel. That wasn't all his fucking hotel. He gave me a share and now he's taken that back. I have to go." And Alex said goodbye to the driver, and stepped out once again on the sidewalk of the most expensive property in the world.

When a woman like Alex became depressed, she went shopping, and that was what Alex had in mind. She remembered this specialty shop around the corner that had women's lingerie along with handcuffs and crops and a few more toys. She'd browsed the store and maybe she'd make some finds she hadn't expected.

It had been a long time since she had to do this kind of shopping. Everything she'd owned had been bought with Max in mind, because he'd been the only man she'd experimented with. He'd been the only man she'd wanted to be involved with, because she didn't come into this world of BDSM because this was something she'd enjoyed. She came into that world because of Max, and now he'd left her alone with no one but his brother. And she thought of Jonas as a brother, and nothing more than that.

However, after what Max had pulled, she felt a strange attraction to Christian with his stunning green eyes, handsome face, wide muscular shoulders, and long legs. *Maybe I can introduce him to something that could take him to a new level in his life,* she thought with a wicked smile playing on her luscious full pink mouth.

———◉———

AFTER BUYING THE SEX toys and outfits Alex needed, which would be her next attack on Max if all else failed, she strolled over to the Millennium Hotel—one of the most expensive and ornate of Max's properties. Alex strutted through the entrance and found the restaurant, but when she walked in, waited in line for service no one recognized her. That could be good, and it could be bad for her.

What could she say, I'm Mrs. Blackstone? "I'm meeting someone for brunch," she said in a small voice. She felt as if she'd lost something by not being the wife of Maximillian Blackstone. Perhaps it was that protective feeling she'd experienced for the time she'd been married to the most powerful man in the world.

Now she felt like an outsider. Max knew what he had done to her once he'd announced to the world that she was no longer his wife.

Alex wanted to cry, but her obstinacy, her steadfast stubborn nature wouldn't let her.

"You have to have a reservation, Ms." The waiter looked over his books, there are no reservations at three o'clock." Then he glanced up at her and over her shoulder, and Alex saw a knowing glance in his eyes.

"But I'm Mrs. Blackstone. Maximillian Blackstone." The waiter's eyes turned back to her.

"Mr. Blackstone isn't married, and if you were indeed her you would know. And may I add, he left explicit orders that if anyone claimed to be Mrs. Blackstone that they were liars and not allowed to enter at any cost."

"She's with me," a low baritone voice echoed. Then a wide smile raced across the host's mouth reaching his eyes, and Alex turned to see Jonas dressed elegantly in a black suit and white shirt no tie. Never had she seen him look so handsome. She'd never looked at Jonas that way before, and she'd forgotten how stunning a man he was when he dressed like Max.

"I'm sorry, Mr. Blackstone, I didn't realize..." The host couldn't stop apologizing. "We have your usual table ready for you. Follow me, please." The host headed to the back of the restaurant where there was a large array of booths.

Since when does Max have a usual table in New York? Alex thought.

Jonas placed his arm around Alex's waist, and they strolled to a booth against the wall where they could watch who came into the dining room. Which was what Max would do at his places of business. After being seated, Alex turned to Jonas.

"Did you know anything about this?" she questioned.

"I thought he'd sold his properties in New York, and especially this hotel. And when did I have time to find out?" Jonas offered Alex an earnest smile. "I've been taking on the part of a father ever since you moved back to Montana. Why didn't you tell Max you wanted to live in a city? You knew you were miserable out there with open range, wild life, and that fucking snow, and you'd never be satisfied anywhere but in a large city. Yet you let him isolate you where you rarely saw anything or anyone, but deer."

When Jonas finished his statement, the waiter was standing patiently waiting for them to order. "I know what I want, I'll have the usual," Jonas said.

"A Porterhouse cooked rare," the waiter repeated as he tapped on a hand computer. Then Jonas realized that he was supposed to be Max, but there was no way he was going to eat a Porterhouse. "No. No. Bring me a New York strip medium to rare. I haven't had a decent New York strip since I left that godforsaken place."

"Since we're eating meat today, I'll have the filet mignon, salad and a shot of Russian vodka. What?" Alex said, looking over at Jonas's expression.

"I've never known you to drink hard liquor, and never vodka," Jonas said after the waiter left them.

"You've never known me to do anything, or be anything but who your brother wanted me to be. Now he wants me to be isolated and alone without money, or his love and protection. Don't be surprised at what I do anymore. There is a change coming, and I don't want to hear from you about what I should or shouldn't do, or what Max wouldn't want. Everyone can do what they want, but when it comes to me, they want to keep me in a box and chained to them, even you, but my chains are broken, and Max was the one who freed me. I bet he didn't know that would be the result. If I know Max, he had something else in mind."

Jonas glanced at Alex, stunned by her admissions.

Chapter 10

After a meal with too many drinks, where Jonas managed to wolf down a large steak with several glasses of Johnny Walker Blue on the rocks as his preferred drink of choice, and lived to talk about it, Alex rose from her seat after her one shot of vodka. "I have to go to the ladies' room."

"Do you want me to go with you?" Alex blinked her eyes at the absurd question.

"Go into the ladies' room with me? Have you lost it? I'm not drunk. I should ask you that question, considering all that you drank."

"I just wanted to make sure you were alright. You seem upset and you haven't eaten anything. I know it's bothering you about Max and your children. You look—"

"Suicidal. Well, you can get that out of your mind. There's no way in hell I'd give Maximillian the opportunity to take my children without a fight. And then there's the matter of all that money that he promised me when I married him. It wasn't for the money that I accepted his proposal. I've never wanted his money. All I've ever wanted was Maximillian—until now. So, sit back and enjoy your drink because I promise you, I won't be doing anything that stupid."

Jonas knew there was nothing reckless about Alex, after all she'd been the most focused, even more focused than Max, but she'd been looking frail lately, eating very little, and he thought perhaps what Max had done to her had chipped away at her strong nature.

There came a time when enough pressure was placed on anything, for example, when a tornado passed through, the way Max had passed through Alex's life, and put the ultimate pressure on her where she'd either break, or weathered the storm called Maximillian Blackstone.

Few had survived even the least amount of pressure whenever Max chose to apply it.

Jonas just wanted to be there if she fell, so he could catch her as she'd done with him many times in his life.

Alex strolled away from the table, headed for the ladies' room tucked discreetly in the back near one of Max's offices. She remembered it was there when she'd accompanied Max one year.

She hoped they hadn't turned that room into a lounge for the employees as he'd discussed doing. As she neared the area, she recalled that in that particular hall, hidden away, was a private dining area where maybe a few others knew where that elaborate room was concealed.

When Max didn't want anyone to see him, and he'd been hungry and had visitors to discuss business over lunch or dinner, he'd have his driver let him and his party out in the back of the hotel.

As Alex strolled in the path of the restroom, something caught her eyes, and the familiar sound of a distinct baritone voice laughing. Alex stopped in her tracks. She turned in the direction of this laughter and headed to the dim-lit room, remembering the booth that she and Max had dined in years before, and in that booth sat Maximillian with a blonde.

They were leaning into each other talking and chuckling out loud. Two waiters stood nearby in case Max and his guest needed anything. All he had to do was raise his hand, and they anticipated what he wanted, whether a glass of wine, bread or even butter.

Alex glanced at them, remembering when he first brought her there to be alone and to have a quiet dinner with him. She had been so in love the way she still was today, but with one slight problem. Then she was his, and now she belonged to no one.

It was at that moment her face flushed in anger. *Max can laugh and enjoy his life like I never existed? Does he even know the pain of separation I feel from him and my children, or does he even care? The cold-hearted bastard,* she thought.

Alex had to find out just what was so entertaining that it would make him joyful when she was clearly out of *her* mind, upset to the point where she couldn't think, and if she had been able to think, she would have avoided Max at all costs.

Alex strode over to the booth where Max sat with the blonde. She held her head high and sucked in a large breath with her heart hammering in her chest. She had been Mrs. Maximillian Blackstone longer than most, and she'd been the first and had his children to prove it, and nothing would stop her from confronting him today. Not even that little voice that said don't do it.

It felt like a long walk to reach where Max sat, one arm resting behind the blonde. Alex wanted to slow down, collect her thoughts, but her body and mind wouldn't allow that. She found herself standing in front of the two contented people with her sour face, and a cloudy mind. Max's piercing serious eyes locked with her clear-brown ones.

"What are you doing here, Alex?" he said in a shaky surprised voice.

"You have no right to ask me questions anymore. Therefore, I won't ask you what you are doing, because I can see that you are celebrating. Are you celebrating that you've made my life miserable, because, trust me, it won't be for long." In that moment of talk, Alex knew what she had to do.

"This is my—"

"I'm not interested in what the fuck she is to you, Max." The woman raised an eyebrow and stirred nervously in her seat. What did she expect Alex to do? Pull her from that seat next to Max and have a brawl in his restaurant. At another time maybe, but she wouldn't give Max the pleasure of seeing her make a fool of herself fighting over a man who clearly didn't want to be with her.

Max looked at Alex, raised an eyebrow, and tightened his jaw with a disapproving glance. "Why are your words so coarse and not at all indicative of the woman I once called my wife, or the mother of my children?"

Alex bristled at his words, furrowed her brow, and narrowed her glance, and said, "You don't get to ask me why I'm suddenly using the F bomb outside our bedroom. You didn't seem to mind when I asked you to *fuck* me."

"If I remember that correctly you begged me," Max added, with a chuckle and a grin that reached up at the corner of his sexy mouth. A mouth that had been between her legs, and brought her to orgasm over and over in the course of a night.

"I think you begged me to tie you up and whip your ass before that occurred. In which case you will want to beg me again, and—"

"There you are, Alex. I was worried about—" Jonas stood in disbelief. Clearly he didn't know when he'd spoken to Max that Max had been in New York all along.

"Jack, you know my brother Jonas," Max said, referring to his secretary. "I think you two were good friends once." That was a surprise to Alex. Those kinds of surprises were coming fast and furious lately.

"Yes, Jacqueline how are you?" Jonas said, and then nodded.

"Good to see you again, Jonas."

"Before you fall into this mutual admiration thing," Alex barked, walked close to Jonas and looked at him, and then Max. "So, this is Jack your secretary. You didn't tell me she was a woman. You and Jonas knew this and kept this from me?"

"I didn't think you wanted to concern yourself with my business," Max responded quickly, if not delicately.

"Is it your thoughts that I didn't want to concern myself with my children as well? Are you just going to let this woman come in and be a mother to my children, and where are they now?"

"They are well taken care of, Alex. And no one is taking over your job as a mother."

"So now it's a job being a mother. That I agree, but it is much more, and they will not accept anyone but me, even if you've found no use for me anymore."

Alex turned to meet Jonas's eyes. "Maybe someone else will discover that I am just what he needs after all. I'll see you in court, Maximillian." And Alex marched off in the direction of the restroom leaving Jonas standing to talk to a nervous and irate Max.

Max raised his hand for a drink, and banged his fist on the table when the drink didn't come fast enough.

Chapter 11

Alex rushed to the restroom, because she didn't want Max to see her cry and get another win. She didn't wait long enough, because she would have understood from Max's behavior that he hadn't won this round.

She'd never cried like this before. Not in her darkest moments when she realized that she'd been adopted, she thought her mother didn't want her, and when she discovered that her mother had died, and she'd never see her face except in a picture.

Alex didn't cry when she met Max and fell in love with him, and realized that she had to raise a child on her own, and when Max discovered that he was a father, he had tried to take her son from her, and she never cried then. But now was different, she felt broken, and she had to do something to heal.

Leaning over and looking at herself in the mirror, she passed her finger under her wet eyes where tears had pooled, and she wiped away her smudged makeup.

Then she straightened her dress, herself, and strolled out with her head up only to see Jonas waiting in a corner near the door. He'd startled her for a second in the dim-lit corridor.

"I thought I would have to go in there after you," Jonas confessed.

"There is no need for you to come to my rescue. There's no one to rescue me from a man the likes of Max," Alex moaned, meeting Jonas's worried eyes. "You could have told me how ruthless he was."

"I thought you knew." Jonas placed his arm around her shoulder. "Let's go. I don't want him angry at me any more than he is. The dinner is on Maximillian since everyone thinks I'm him," Jonas chuckled.

Jonas and Alex strolled to the front and out of the restaurant, and out of the hotel into the bright fading sunlight. Alex glanced over at Jonas, "You do clean up well." Then as they were stepping to raise their hands for a cab, a limo pulled up and the window lowered.

"I was shopping, and I thought you might need a ride home."

Jonas brow furrowed. "Were you having us followed?"

"I wouldn't think of following you, Jonas. Maybe that beautiful woman, but never you," Christian said with a wide closed smile.

"Yes, I would like a ride home," Alex admitted. Christian's driver exited the limo and rushed around to the door and opened it, then stood in the way when Jonas made an attempt to get into the car.

Jonas stooped to get a glance at Alex sitting next to Christian, hoping she'd protest, but she didn't. "You can take a cab, Jonas," Alex said, and she sat back where all Jonas saw was Christian's smug face. It was then Jonas questioned the wisdom of introducing her to him.

Looking straight ahead, Alex said in a cool voice, "Jonas, take a cab and I'll be home shortly. Don't worry, I'm safe with Christian. There's no need to wait up for me."

"I thought we were going to see a real-estate agent. You know the hotel is temporary," Jonas noted.

"We will, but not today," Alex assured, just in case Jonas didn't hear her. However, he'd heard her, but didn't want to.

Christian turned away from Alex to shoot Jonas a nasty sneer, and then raised the darkened window.

When Christian's limo drove off into the evening traffic, Max's limo pulled up and Jonas stood bewildered. He wondered if he should tell his brother, or get into a cab and mind his own business. But Alex and Max were his business, and both of them were heading down a cliff they weren't prepared for.

Just as Jonas raised his hand to hail a cab, Max stepped out of his hotel, engrossed in talk with Jacqueline. Then Jonas locked eyes with Max as he neared the limo. "Can I give you a ride Jonas?"

Jonas's first thought was, *How can Max be so cool after his encounter with Alex?* One minute Max was clearly uneasy, and that was when he thought it best to leave him and find Alex in the restroom. Now Max appeared as if nothing bothered him.

However, Jonas knew Max's secrets.

Jonas knew how much Max loved Alex before all this shit went down. Could he be as heartless and cold as Alex thought? Could Max have moved on? Maybe there was room in Alex's life for him since Max no longer wanted her in his. He'd thought as much since Alex implied that someone would want her if Max didn't, and he wanted to be that man when she turned to someone else.

"Don't think I don't know what the fuck you're doing, Max?"

"Jacqueline, please get into the car. I have to talk to Jonas. This won't take long." Max helped Jacqueline into the car and then turned quickly on the ball of his feet to meet Jonas with a growl. "What the fuck do you want, Jonas?"

"I want to know why you're treating Alex the way you are. Don't you see how much she loves you? Do you have to take everything from her to realize that you are everything to her, you and her children?"

"She is my wife—"

Jonas interrupted Max, "She's no longer your wife, and if you weren't so narrow focused, jealous, and vindictive, you could see what you are doing to all of us, especially her. I'll be alright even without you, but all she had was her children because I see now she doesn't have you and never did. No one could break through that exterior of yours. I thought maybe she had, and you were human, but I know now that you are as cold as that man she left with in his limo."

"Who are you talking about? Where is Alex?" Max's body twisted to the left and right. Jonas finally saw Max's cold exterior break like pieces of a polar cap. "Are you going to tell me who Alex left with?"

"Christian Kenley."

"Isn't he—once she discovers the truth about him she won't be there long." Max turned to stroll in the direction of his limo, before Jonas reached and caught his arm. Max turned with a sour look meeting Jonas's eyes.

"Don't walk away from me, Max. You're going to hear me out." Max didn't move and he didn't say a word. He knew when Jonas was like this, it was best that he listened.

"Christian Kenley asked Alex to marry him on their first meeting."

"I suppose you were the one to introduce them."

"I will not lie to you Max. I was the one only because we didn't have any access to money, and you cut both of us off. What the fuck did you want us to do?"

Max watched Jonas and they both raked their fingers through their hair at the same time. It was something they did as young boys when they were nervous, and thought their father would punish them after they'd gone off and decided that they didn't want to return home. They were going to run away, become stowaways on a boat and see the world.

"You are responsible for this, Jonas," Max barked.

"Don't blame me for your fucked-up thinking." Max turned and headed to his limo and opened the door and climbed in. Then he hit a button and the window lowered. "You'd better not let anything happen to Alex. You're responsible for bringing her back to *us*." And Max's limo pulled out and left Jonas thinking about what Max had said.

Now he's holding me responsible for his fucked-up decisions. I'll be damned if I let him get away with this. She's not my wife, he thought.

When Jonas entered the cab, Christian's limo was pulling up to his apartment with Alex.

Chapter 12

Alex glanced at Christian as they walked into his elevator. She couldn't help thinking how handsome a man he was. Couldn't he have found him someone that would meet his sexual needs? She didn't like him that way. But he was charming, and maybe she could learn to like him, or even love him someday if she'd give herself a chance. After all, she loathed Max now, and she would try everything in her power to hurt him. She hated him, and she hated herself for wanting him more now than before.

"What?" Alex questioned, when she saw Christian staring at her when the door to the elevator opened into Christian's penthouse apartment.

"I'm thinking that if you were mine, I would want no one else in my life, nor would I need someone else. Only you." Alex moved to the sofa overlooking the Manhattan skyline and sat. Christian sat beside her. "I sensed with our talk on our way here that you were considering my proposal of marriage."

"I was just thinking that maybe we could enter into a contract for a short time, and we could renew it if it wasn't conducive to our needs. Or my needs."

"What is it that you propose, Alex?" He reached for her hands and Alex let him. He turned her palms up and leaned and kissed them. She thought she would be repulsed by the feel of another man's mouth and hand over hers, but she wasn't.

There was a heat in his touch which traveled through her, she felt aroused and a calming effect that she never felt with Max. Max had her upset most of the time because he'd leave her, and it always had to do with his business. And she'd feel alone.

Max would leave her with Jonas. Now she realized that Jonas was more of a watchdog, and he wasn't a good one at that.

"I need you not for what you think. I don't want to lie to you. I want my children back, and if it is possible, I want my husband back," Alex said, peering into Christian's understanding eyes.

"I need you also. I haven't been this open with a woman before for fear that she would leave me, and when it came down to telling her what she would be facing if she married me, I discovered that she'd leave me anyway."

Alex stared thinking about Christian. Why would a woman leave this obviously handsome man who appeared to need love and appeared to be from her observation—caring and kind?

"The way it looks, I think we need each other. Can we come together in a partnership of some kind, and try to make each other happy for as long as possible? I will never force you to stay with me, and I don't want your pity. If you agree to be with me, promise me that it wouldn't be out of pity."

Christian leaned to kiss Alex and she moved away. "I will never be with a man because of pity, and, I think it's way too early to think about you and me together. We should take this slow?"

"Do you think you have much time when it comes to Maximillian? Do you think he's taking anything slow? He got a divorce from you before you could fly here to New York when it was almost impossible to obtain a divorce that quick. He's probably trying to figure out a way to keep your children from seeing you. I know Maximillian, and he's a very deliberate and thorough man. Once he discovers that you're with me, he will use everything in his power to destroy both of us. He owns powerful men. He would probably say the same thing of me," Christian added.

Alex sat thinking and trying to wrap her head around Christian's words. *He knew Maximillian well, perhaps better than me. He must have had some dealings with him because Max had his hands in a lot of business deals and companies, and with Jonas helping him by substituting as Max, Max was able to control most of his companies, but now with Jonas out of the picture he had to be vulnerable,* Alex thought.

Alex didn't want to see the man she loved destroyed, unless she was the one to destroy him, and then when he rose from his ashes she wanted it to be her who brought him back. Maybe then he'd understand that she had to be respected as his wife, his partner, and mother to his children.

This was her desire, but could she pull it off? Christian had been talking to Alex and she was drowning in her thoughts when she heard Christian's voice, and it brought her back to the here and now.

"It's never too early or late for me to be with you. I've wanted you from the time I saw your picture in the newspapers. I've loved you from that one glance, and I can't believe that you're with me now. Would it be too early to tell you that I love you, and if you marry me I'll do everything I can to make you happy?"

"It's never too early for that, but first I must warn you that I need my children with me."

"It will be done." Just like that. What did Christian know or have on Max where he'd been confident that he could take him on?

"You sound sure of yourself, Christian. What do you have that will overcome what Max is doing or has done?"

"Money. I have more money than he has. I have more judges, senators than he has. I have more resources than he will ever have, and I'm younger than he is. And I have his greatest resource sitting near me. Maybe *you* one day." Christian aimed a wide knowing smile at Alex, and she felt secure in that smile and his warm touch as he laid his palm over her hand, took it, turned it over and kissed the inside of her hands once more.

"If I were to agree to marry you, where would we live? I mean with my children."

"Does this place look like it won't accommodate children?" Christian said with a laugh. Alex glanced around at the ornate antiques, white colored furniture throughout. The expensive rugs and paintings.

"No, don't answer that, it was the wrong question." Christian turned to Alex with a warm smile. "However, I will promise you one thing, they will have a home where they can be happy."

"My children need wide open spaces. They are used to a country life, not living in a city since they are old enough to go to school."

"I know your concerns and I do promise you that you will be able to choose where we live. When you have had enough of Max controlling your life, and trying to wreak havoc on it just call me, and I'll be waiting. I have nothing better to do. I'll wait for you a lifetime if I have to."

That statement Christian made took Alex's breath away.

Chapter 13

When Alex walked up to the door of her hotel suite, opened the door, but before she could lay her purse down and kick off her shoes, Jonas met her on her way to her room. "Where have you been?"

"Seriously, Jonas? Are you questioning me? Max didn't question me like that?"

"Maybe he should have?"

"Have you turned against me, too? All I can say is not today. I'm not any mood for some more of the Blackstone macho bullshit." Alex pushed past Jonas and turned away from her room, then sauntered into the living area to drop her purse on a bar near the butler's sink.

"I'm just saying he shouldn't have allowed you to go off and get involved with me." Alex's mouth fell open, and she narrowed her eyes at Jonas.

"I can't believe what you're saying. Do you mean to tell me that you've finally realized that you are the cause of my marriage falling apart? Think about it, Jonas. He sent me to you, remember. He sent me to you to learn how to become a Dominatrix for him, as well as a submissive."

"Yes, I remember, but can we forget that for now. Max is the reason all this shit is happening. He had been too busy and wouldn't give up his businesses, not even for his children and wife. Now he's thrown you away for the predators to come in and pick you apart."

"I don't want to hear any more of this." She turned away from Jonas, and went where she'd initially wanted to go in the first place—her bedroom. She felt like climbing in bed and never getting out.

Alex sat on the bench at the foot of her bed, and removed her shoes, then she looked over at Jonas who'd sat in a chair across from her.

"What do you mean predators will pick me apart? Are you talking about Christian? If you are, you are wrong. Christian is a beautiful soul—"

Jonas interjected before Alex continued. "Waiting to take over *your* soul." Jonas's eyes met Alex's when she looked across at him.

"You must be talking about your brother. He took over my soul and body with his bondage, and we won't discuss what all he didn't want or do to me. Now get out of here. I need to go to bed," Alex barked.

"I'm going to leave, but you need to know that Max loves you in his own way."

"Well, he has a hell of a way of showing it. I don't want to talk any more about Max or Christian, or you."

"Just look at your phone, Alex. He's been calling and texting you. And when he couldn't get you to answer, he contacted me, and I had to tell him that you were with Christian Kenley. Then he came to his senses. He realized that he could lose you. Max has always been impulsive, jealous, and covetous of what he loved, to the point—"

"Where he'd break his toys if they didn't perform the way he'd wanted them to." Jonas aimed a telling glare at Alex. That was exactly what Alex thought, and she wanted no part of Max now.

That sealed it for her. She would entertain Christian until she could make up her mind whether she wanted to marry him or not. Maybe not having a sexual relationship with a man would do her body and mind some good. She needed a rest from the sexual bondage she'd enjoyed with Maximillian.

"Close the door on your way out, Jonas. I'm taking a shower. I think I need a long one after tonight."

"I'm going to a club," Jonas stated as he strode to the door.

"This late? The only clubs that are open are private clubs," Alex noted, and with a knowing glance she slanted her head, and when Jonas didn't say a word, she knew where he was going. "Close the door on your way out," she repeated with a stern voice.

Jonas wanted Alex to say something to stop him.

What could she say to him to stop him from his life? It wasn't her responsibility to prevent him from going to a bondage club. Maybe he needed what she'd provided to his brother, Max. Maybe it was the only thing to make him functional. She didn't know, and at that moment she didn't care. She'd had too much of the Blackstone men to last a lifetime.

Heaven knows she couldn't flog his ass until he'd cum. That had only been reserved for Max.

Who is servicing Max now? Alex wondered. Maybe it was that blonde she'd seen him with. Alex had been Max's saving grace, and now he was out there for a woman to claim him, because she was no longer his wife, and he'd declared to the world and himself that she was of no use to him by his objectionable behavior. Well, he'd made his choice, and perhaps he thought that he didn't need Alex anymore.

Time would tell.

Chapter 14

Alex thought she'd been dreaming when she heard a buzzer, as if it was stuck. Then a loud ring, then a pause, and the ringing started again over and over, and she wondered why someone didn't get the door. Finally, she sat up, glanced around, looked out at the buildings and realized where she was, and it wasn't a dream, but a nightmare that she was still in a hotel and not in her bed at her home.

She'd fallen asleep after a shower, and crawled under the covers naked, the way she used to do when Max was due to come home from one of his overseas trips.

Stepping to the floor, rushing to see who was constantly ringing the bell, and why Jonas hadn't answered by now because he was a light sleeper, she panicked, questioning if something had happened to Jonas.

Alex searched around for her robe. She found the nearest one, shrugged her arms through a robe that the hotel had provided, and hurried to Jonas's room. He wasn't there. Perhaps he'd forgotten his key. No, that wasn't it, he could have gotten one at the desk.

Then who the fuck is it? she wondered. She opened the door without looking through the peephole.

When she pulled the door open, standing in front of her was Max. Her heart hammered in her chest, her eyes brightened, and she almost smiled with relief, but she didn't want to show any emotions, so she schooled them back, furrowed her brow, and said, "What do you want?"

"I want to come in." Max's voice was deep and sexy, his eyes roving over her from her hair to her breasts.

Her breathing accelerated, and her mind begged her not to let him in, but her heart weakened and said differently, and she stood back, with Max locking eyes with hers. He sauntered inside as if he had her under a spell like a cat would do with a mouse.

She was his now, but the spell was quickly broken when the oxygen returned to her brain.

"Do you know what time it is?" Alex barked, after crossing her arms over her breasts.

"Yes. But I couldn't sleep," Max admitted.

"And how is that my problem now?" Alex questioned.

"I am your problem. We have children together, and—"

Alex stopped Max in mid-conversation. "You've taken my children."

"I'll let you see them if you come back to me."

What the fuck? Alex thought. "Did I miss something? Am I in a parallel universe where there are two Maximillians? You divorced me without me having anything to say about that, and then I see you sitting and enjoying a conversation with a woman, your secretary who you called Jack. Leading me to believe that she was a man. What do you say about that?"

"I didn't think you knowing that my secretary was a woman would affect you. It was just business, Alex."

"Like you and me."

"Nothing is like you and me," Max said, and when she watched Max look down and pass his tongue over his lips, his eyes half-lidded, she realized that her robe had fallen open,, and when she reached to tie the belt, he caught her hand.

His head lowered, and before she could resist or say *no*, he had his warm mouth suckling her breasts, her nipples exploding in his mouth, and his hand between her legs as his finger brushed over her clit. The heat of his body close to hers, his large hands palming her mound, as her hips shot forward and her juice dripping down on Max's finger as he pushed it in and pulled it out of her opening.

When Max pulled his mouth from her breasts, and his finger from her pussy, a gasp fell from her mouth and her legs weakened and she fell into his arms. All she remembered was that he was carrying her somewhere, and when he kicked open her bedroom door and entered it, he laid her on the bed ever so gently.

She heard him toe off his shoes, open the belt to his pants, move his zipper downward, and the thump of his pants being thrown across the bench. She saw him lean over her naked, and he laid his powerful chest over her. She felt him help her take off her robe, and say, "Magnificent. I will never let anyone have you."

Alex should have known something then, but she was too much in love with Max to care what he'd said. She just wanted to feel him near her. She'd missed looking into his stunning face, as she passed her hands over his stubbled jaw. Now, at this time, she didn't care how or why he was there, because she wanted and needed him.

Therefore, when he eased down her body after sucking her breasts hard, his tongue licking down her body, his large hands opening her legs as his tongue licked along her folds, and then her clit, and her wet opening. Alex let out a moan of pleasure and screamed Max's name as she reached and took a handful of his silky dark hair.

Alex opened her legs wide as Max's tongue massaged her clit until she was ready. "Max, fuck me," Alex screamed once again. He acted as if he didn't hear her, and continued licking, sucking, and kissing her tender clit, torturing her as she squirmed, and twisted with her legs wrapped firmly around his slim waist.

Alex was ready, and heated beyond her imagination. She dug her fingers into Max's shoulders breaking his skin. He leaned up and gazed at her. She was indeed vulnerable again. Not that woman in the restaurant who'd threatened him, and walked away, but so was Max.

Alex could feel Max's pre-cum-covered cock rub against her leg as he placed his muscular arms on both sides of her, where she could look into his eyes.

She saw lust, desire, love, but she couldn't figure out the smirk on his face as he reached for his full heavy cock and stroked it, lined it up with her quivering opening, and said, "Baby, feel me, and don't ever forget what I feel like." And when he shoved his length into her body she knew that she would never forget this night.

The moment Max entered her tight opening, her orgasm couldn't be contained, and it covered his hard shaft, and he said, "I feel you, Alex. Your tight pussy squeezing my cock. That's what I've always known about you, you were the only woman who could make me feel something. I need you. I need you to make me feel again. I thought I could do without you, but now I know that I can't."

Alex wanted Max, but she didn't hear what she wanted. She wanted an apology for making her feel alone and thrown away by him. She wanted an apology for taking her children and she wanted most of all to hear that he loved her the way she loved him.

Predictably, she didn't get it, but she knew one thing for sure that before she'd go back to him if he asked her, it would be on her terms.

Another thing that was inescapable was that Max couldn't live without her, and she had to make him see that. Was he that arrogant and narcissistic to believe that it was all about him, and all he had to do was make love to her and all would be forgotten?

She knew that if she gave him what he needed this night, she was on her way to bringing Maximillian to his knees in more ways than he'd anticipated.

"Turn on your stomach," he demanded. *Still playing the game of Dominant*, she thought. She would play his games, but she had a few of her own.

Alex rolled over as he sat on his haunches. Then he reached and placed his finger inside her wet soggy opening filled with his cum, and without out the tightness of before, Max leaned up and filled her once more with his thick magnificent cock.

Holding Alex with his hand underneath her stomach, pounding into her opening, she thought it unusual that he wanted only her pussy, when he'd been a man who wanted everything from her.

His desires were insatiable. His sexual needs boarded on the extreme, and she had been up to the task since she'd married Maximillian Blackstone.

He'd spanked her with his strong palm until her ass was red, and he'd come all over her ass from seeing his handywork. She'd tied him up, teased his cock, sucked him off until she thought he couldn't cum any more, but he'd look up at her with half-lidded eyes, his legs and arms held by restraints, and said, 'More. Give me *more* of the same, and this time whip me harder.'

To Alex's surprise this time he insisted that he'd fuck her first, and he did. The night had gone, and he was still inside her opening and Alex had lost count of how many times they'd both come.

Max roused from his sleep, Alex's head on his chest, and he asked, "Do you have any restraints, or a belt, I need something now. I need you to punish me the way you used to as my Dominatrix. I'm out of control. Don't you know how much I've wanted you?"

No, Alex didn't know. He hadn't made that known lately. All she felt from him was anger and resentment for her trying to help out Jonas. She wanted to have a discussion with Max. *Maybe they could see a family therapist to iron out their disagreements. It had worked before why not now,* she thought.

Alex wanted this badly, so she could get home to her children, and salvage their marriage. The way Max had taught her to make love to him, and he to her, who else could compete with what Max had taught her sexually to enjoy? How could she even get used to another man the way she'd become?

Alex wasn't used to a normal sexual relationship with a man. Max had been her first love, her first man, and she thought he would be her last. *How could I adjust to a normal life if there was none with Maximillian?* she wondered.

Chapter 15

The sex had been wonderful, but there was something missing and Alex knew it. Maybe she would find it now that Max had asked her to be his Dominatrix once more if only for tonight. Maybe he'd realized that she was the only woman who could satisfy him.

It had been fortuitous that she'd found a shop that sold her what she needed. Alex didn't know that she would need these things this soon, but she believed that one day Max would come to her because after all, try as he might, he'd never found another woman who could give him what he needed in so many ways.

When Max had lain on his stomach and she'd reached for the package in the drawer, she pulled out of the bag, a crop, handcuffs, and leather restraints. She wished she had her whip and a cane, because she wanted to give him a few lashes on his hard-firm ass, and maybe the tip of his penis or his balls. The sting from her whip always brought his cock to life after a long session, or after he'd returned home spent from traveling and too many meetings.

Crawling across Max's superb muscular body, she tied his wrists first, and then his ankles. She wouldn't use the handcuffs unless she had to. "I want you to lie there and don't say a word. If I hear you protest or cry out, I'm going to abuse you more in ways you've never experienced," Alex whispered into his ear, as she leaned over his back brushing her nipples over his skin, watching goosebumps rise as she moved down between his legs.

"Alex—"

"Quiet," she barked. "If you speak and call my name again, I will take the restraints off and you can leave, and go to whoever you want. I don't care anymore." But in reality Alex did care. She cared too much for Maximillian, and she'd hoped for this day when he'd come to her instead of seeking out someone else to relieve his sexual desires.

Looking at Max's body, strong and lean, *what a magnificent man*, she thought. And he was no longer her husband. In dismay and resentment, Alex aimed the crop, started at his waist and trailed it slowly down to his buttocks, raised it, and with the flick of her wrist she brought the crop down on his ass brutally over and over.

Max tried to reach for his cock, but he'd been restrained from doing so. Those were his wishes because he didn't want any artificial stimulation. He wanted and needed Alex to bring him to orgasm with what she'd been capable of doing before.

After dotting Max's ass with lashes of her crop, and when it turned red she knew he'd had enough and was ready for her to suck him off.

She untied his wrists and ankles, and when he once more lay on his back, and looked down on her, she barked, "Don't look at me. Or I'll blindfold you. And don't touch me." Max averted his eyes upward as Alex leaned over him, with her full breasts dragging along his body. Her taut nipples trailed over his lips where he opened his mouth.

She quickly pulled them away, and continued down his body as she reached for his cock and stroked it from the base to the tip, and then she opened her mouth and took his thick full erect cock into her warm mouth.

Alex heard a sigh of relief, a moan of pleasure.

A taste of pre-cum fell on her tongue. It tasted familiar. It tasted like Max. Alex sucked his cock hard, and took it down her throat without gagging, and Max remembered to stay still and not move, because the feeling had been wonderful.

Max had an inclination to grab his length, and help place it in Alex's mouth when she pulled her face away, but he knew if he did that she would stop at that moment and he would be left frustrated, and he didn't want to enrage Alex, because he didn't want to go to anyone, but her.

How could he have been so short-sighted as to pull a stunt the way he did? Get a divorce when he knew deep down he'd needed Alex just to breathe, just to carry on with his life, and not to mention his sexual desires which were a great part of living in this chaotic world of being a Blackstone.

He had to tell her that he was wrong, but he couldn't talk, she'd forbade him to say a word otherwise she'd put him out, and all that would have been his fault. Now he had to lie still and let Alex work her magic on his body where he'd be able to rest and sleep to carry on what he had to do the next day.

And rest he did with her lying on his chest, and his cum all over her.

———— ◉ ————

WHEN HIS PHONE RANG, he was stepping out of the shower, and Alex was still asleep. He moved to the next room to answer it, and not disturb her. He had meetings today, and he was ready after what had happened last night. Max knew now what had to be done.

"There's a problem at one of your plants in Hong Kong, and you have to fly over there today," his secretary insisted.

"Can't the plant manager handle it, Jack?"

"No. Only you can clear up the problem with the personnel. They want to see your face and talk to you." Max knew he should have closed that plant or sold it years ago. Alex had been right. There was no way he could sustain a marriage and be there for his children with the kind of schedule he'd had, and with all these properties and businesses, and everything had become far worse now that he'd sent Jonas away.

Jonas had been a stand in, and since they looked undistinguishable from each other, he'd sent Jonas to his overseas plants, but he didn't have that cover anymore and that was another thing he had regretted—sending his brother away.

"I'll be at the airfield in twenty minutes." Max looked at Alex lying naked, and he moaned. He had to leave her once more when he had so much to confess, tell her, beg her to forgive him, but like always, he didn't have the time.

He didn't even have time to leave her one of his infamous notes. Max rushed out of the hotel, climbed into his limo waiting, and parked on the ramp in front of the hotel door.

⸻ ◉ ⸻

WHEN MAX WAS BOARDING his private jet headed to Hong Kong, Jonas was entering a cab with two girls from a club. For once he took Alex's advice and had not gone to a BDSM club. He felt that this would be safer than being tied up and maybe left in some hotel room all night and have the maid find them and it would end up in the papers the next day.

He could see the headlines: ***Maximillian's Bad Boy Twin Handcuffed to a Bed in one of his Millennium Hotels.*** *TMS would have a field day with those pictures and video,* he thought, so he sauntered into a club near one of his favorite BDSM spots.

And now Jonas was headed to a party at a one of the girls' boyfriend's apartment. Jonas met the girls on the dim-lit dance floor, where he inserted himself in the middle of their gyration, their bumping and grinding on each other. He didn't know their names and he wasn't interested in finding out who they were because he was looking for one thing, and that was, when the fuck was he going to get laid?

On entering the apartment, one girl introduced Jonas to the crowd of drunken young men and women in their early twenties. The men remarked in a joke that Jonas might have been past his bedtime. But the girls said they wanted him there because he was handsome, and they liked men in their thirties because they were more mature.

Jonas probably should have known better than to party with a bunch of entitled out-of-control twenty-something girls and guys. After all, he'd been one himself, and it got him into all kinds of trouble.

Nevertheless, he decided to stay at least until he could get one or two of the girls to give him a blow job, and another later for him to fuck.

As Jonas sauntered through the crowd, he watched some of them smoking and drinking, and he thought some were using drugs. He'd been drunk most of the day even after declaring that he was off the stuff, but with all the shit that had gone on in his life with his wife being dead, Alex appearing to not want him around, and his brother Max thinking that he was useless, he needed something to ease his pain, and so he drank hard liquor for the first time in months.

With his hands over the girl's shoulder, Jonas whispered in her ear, "Can we go someplace where we can be alone?"

"Sure." And she led him into a room at the far end of the hall. They closed the door and didn't lock it. Jonas in his inebriated state, fell across the bed, and all he felt and heard was his zipper easing down, and his pants being pulled past his ass.

Jonas did remember the girl saying, "Nice cock and a thick long one. I can't wait to get that inside me."

When the girl sat on his cock, and pushed it inside her, he felt it come alive, and he reached and placed his hands on her hips. He punched his hips upward, and now with a stiff erection, he let her ride him rough, biting, scratching, and bringing him to orgasm.

After a much-needed release he felt her body leave him, and that was when he fell asleep.

When he woke, the police was standing over him. "Wake up. Wake the fuck up. You're being arrested."

In his bleary-eyed state and a muddled mind Jonas ask, "What did I do?" when the police handcuffed him and marched him out half-naked, his zipper undone, in front of a crowd of strangers he'd only met last night.

"There's a woman dead in the alley, and you were the last one to see her alive," one police officer barked. The only thought Jonas had was, *This can't be happening.*

Chapter 16

Alex woke in the middle of the day hungry like she'd never been before, and sore and tired. She glanced over at the spot where Max had lain, aware that Max had come to her last night, and what had transpired between the two.

Her thought was that he couldn't have left her when he knew how important the night had been for the both of them. She wanted to wake up in his arms and know his commitment to them getting back together, and her seeing her children. She wanted to hear him tell her how much he loved her.

Strutting to the shower with Max's dried cum on her body, she needed a shower first before anything. Before he looked at her this morning, she wanted to look her best.

Alex had been sure Max hadn't gone too far, because there were none of his fucking notes he'd usually leave beside the bed or on his pillow. And if he had stepped out, he'd be back, because he did say that he wanted to talk to her.

Confident that she and Max would get back together, she strutted to the bathroom, but before she reached it, her phone began ringing and she rushed to pick it up.

"Max?"

"No, it's not Max. It's—"

"I know your voice, Jonas, what is it this time?"

"I'm in trouble."

"What else is new, Jonas? You can't go anywhere without getting in trouble. A man like you should never go out of the house at all," Alex joked.

"This is serious, Alex. I'm at the courthouse now and I'm being charged with murder, and I don't know the woman or whose apartment I was in, or anything." Alex froze. She didn't know what to say. When it reached her brain what Jonas had just said, all she wanted to do was scream: *For fuck's sake, Jonas, not now, and not today*, but she didn't, she just listened.

"I need to make bail and I don't have any money, Alex. The court-appointed attorney is useless. I need a lawyer now. They don't want to give me a low bail because it's murder. I think it's in the millions. The prosecutor doesn't want me to have bail because he said that I'm a flight risk because of the Blackstone name. You know me, Alex," Jonas's voice cracked, "I wouldn't hurt a woman. Never in my life did I touch a woman except for sex, and that's what they said that after I had sex with her, I killed her. That doesn't make any sense."

"Where is Max? Have you called him?" Alex's voice was low.

"I called him first and no answer. I need lots of money to get me out of here, and then my lawyer isn't sure they'll grant me bail. I need Max to help me."

"I'll get you out no matter what I have to do, Jonas. You can count on me. Have I ever let you down?" Alex said, searching around for the remote.

"Never."

"I'll get you bail and a lawyer. Relax and I'll have you out today."

Alex turned around in a circle after her call ended with Jonas. She could hear the panic in his voice. She felt so sorry for him. How had he put himself in such a situation like this? When she turned on the news to try to see if there was any mention of Jonas, not surprising it was all over the news.

A reporter standing in front of the courthouse where they brought Jonas turned to the camera and spoke into a microphone, "Jonas Blackstone the brother of Maximillian Blackstone, the well-known billionaire, has finally gotten himself in trouble that he can't get out of this time even with his brother's help. The police say they have him dead to rights with his DNA all over a dead girl's body. The young woman from a blue-collar family in New Jersey was reported missing a week ago, but was found last night in the alley of an apartment building."

The reporter's camera panned away to show the policeman and several of the young men and women with coats over their heads hiding from their parents, being led away for questioning.

The reporter continued, "Cameras in front of the apartment building showed Jonas Blackstone getting out of a cab with two girls and going into the building, and cameras from another angle had him stepping inside an apartment. There were no cameras at the rear of the apartment building in the alley to show how the girl got there, and how Jonas carried her behind the building and dumped her. Yet the police suspect that he took her down a fire escape leading down to the alley below."

Alex petrified, rushed into the shower for a quick one, and then called Christian. "Can you send a car for me, Christian? I have an emergency. I think I'm too upset to catch a cab. I'd like to talk to you."

"I was wondering when you'd call. I've been watching this all morning on CNN and I want to talk to you as well."

Alex dressed in a hurry, not bothering to eat, and when she walked outside the hotel, Christian's limo was waiting at the entrance.

⎯⎯⎯◦⎯⎯⎯

WHEN THE CAR CAME TO a stop, Alex hurried out of the car, not waiting for Christian's driver to get out and open the door. She found herself in the elevator and stepped out into Christian's penthouse apartment with him standing there waiting.

Alex rushed to Christian, and he held her in his arms. "You're going to be alright, Alex. Everything is going to be alright, sweetheart. I'll do whatever you want to get Jonas out of jail."

Christian led Alex by her hands to the great room overlooking the city. "On my way out of my hotel suite, I think they said that Jonas wasn't granted bail because he's a flight risk and he has money to leave the country. But Jonas has nowhere to go. Can't you understand? He's like a child and he doesn't have Max to depend on."

"Where's Maximillian?" Christian asked, and the way he'd asked that question he knew something, but Alex didn't know what. But then anyone who knew anything about Maximillian Blackstone knew he had to be flying somewhere in the US or to some foreign country. Max never trusted anyone but Jonas to help him, and Max didn't know how to delegate. He had been a hands-on kind of man, and that was why he'd gotten in trouble with his marriage and everything in his life—his health, and his sex life.

"I don't know," Alex said, trying not to answer the question with an excuse. "I tried calling, but he didn't answer." She didn't want to tell Christian about last night, because frankly it wasn't his business.

That was between her and Max.

Besides, she didn't know just what had happened between the two of them. What would she have told him anyway? That he ate her pussy, and she sucked his dick and they fucked and after that she used a crop on his ass to bring about an orgasm, and they both slept soundly holding each other. She slept so soundly that she didn't hear him sneak out of her bed.

When Alex woke he was gone. Disappeared in his usual manner. Nothing had changed when she'd been hoping something would, considering that they were so far apart, and they'd never had a gap in their relationship the likes of the Grand Canyon.

"If you want me to call up someone, I will, and I'll have Jonas out in a matter of hours, but I want something in return."

Alex glanced over at Christian with a knowing glance. What could he want? A kiss, a date? That would be easy. She'd go out on a real date with him. Why not? She was free to date others until she and

Max married again. He was a gorgeous young man, tall, with a beautiful body like Max's. The only differences were Max had equipment to have sex with her, and since she wasn't interested in having sex with anyone but Max, then she thought nothing of repaying him with a kind gesture.

Alex turned to Christian with a relaxed smile on her face. "What is it that you want? Do you want me to date you? I'd be happy to go on a date."

"I want more than that." *What more could he want?* Alex thought. She agreed that a date was nothing if he'd get a judge and a good lawyer to handle Jonas's case. He might need a private detective too. Therefore, Alex sat back and listened to what Christian wanted.

"I want you to marry me."

"You want what?" She moved away from Christian to see if he was joking, but he wasn't laughing. He was more than serious, and it appeared that his smooth forehead furrowed, and his eyes narrowed when her voice appeared to rise in annoyance.

"I'm serious, Alex. You must have known where this was headed. You're a smart woman. If that is the only way I can have a woman like you as my own, then these are my terms. You have to marry me, or I will not do it."

"Are you blackmailing me? Because if you are, I will never consent to something like that. If I were to marry you it would have to be on my own terms."

"You mistake my intentions. This is not a bribe or extortion it is a contract we will enter into. If I get Jonas out and I do all the things to make this case go away, then you have to marry me, or he will rot in jail. Do you think Max will get here in time to keep him out of Rikers Island? A rich man like him will die there or worse, and we don't want to discuss what is worse."

Alex stood and marched to the terrace door. Then she turned, and with a sour look said, "I'll marry you. I'll do anything to keep Jonas out of jail. Can you get him out tonight?"

"I'll not only get him out tonight, but I can get the charges thrown out. But you have to marry me tonight on my yacht. My captain will marry us, and then I'll call my lawyers and the judge that I know who owes me a favor, and Jonas will be a free man."

Chapter 17

When Jonas stumbled out of jail with his designer suit dusty and dirty, his white shirt torn and soiled, his wrist from the handcuffs red and sore, state of mind demoralized, the captain of Christian's yacht was marrying Alex and Christian.

Jonas looked to the lawyer Christian had sent to expedite his case, took a deep breath and asked, "Can I use your phone to call my sister-in-law Alexander Blackstone? I have to tell her I'm out of jail, and to thank her for what she'd done for me, and that I'll arrive at the hotel in fifteen minutes."

"You should do more than thank her," the lawyer advised, reaching into his front pocket and handing Jonas the phone. "You might need to call someone else to give them that good news."

Jonas reached for the phone, but before he punched in the numbers he looked over at the lawyer who had to be in his late sixties with a shock of grey hair, a man who had seen too many courtrooms at this time of night, and had argued too many cases in his lifetime.

"What do you mean I should call someone else?" Jonas questioned.

"I didn't say that. What I meant was, you can't call her, and I don't think she's anywhere close enough to the mainland where she can get your call," the attorney said, as they stepped outside the courtroom heading in the direction of the waiting limo.

Jonas stopped, then turned to face the lawyer. "Do you know where Alex Blackstone is? Well, you must." Jonas narrowed his eyes and furrowed his brow waiting for the attorney to tell him what he didn't know.

"It's my understanding—" He gazed at his watch. "—she's no longer Alexander Blackstone, but Mrs. Kenley by now, and she's sailing away to some island for her honeymoon."

"Are you fucking kidding me?" Jonas barked.

"I'm a serious man, and if there's one thing I don't do this time of night is to make fucking jokes. She married Christian as a stipulation that he'd get you out of jail, and have the charges dismissed. She signed a contract and it's binding. I can show it to you if you'd like. I'd say she loves you very much. Knowing your reputation, Jonas Blackstone, I'd say she loves you a fucking hell of a lot. Oh, Christian is a young good-looking man, but he will never be able to be a husband to her. I hope she knows this and knows who she's dealing with."

The attorney headed for the limo and climbed in. Jonas stood in one spot trying to wrap his brain around why Alex would do such a thing. "I don't have all night, Jonas, are you coming?" the lawyer bellowed.

Jonas with a dark look in his otherwise bright eyes, ambled in the direction of the limo and climbed inside and closed the door, asked for a drink, and the driver angled the car off into the traffic.

Of course, Alex knew what Christian was, or thought she'd known, and she'd married him anyway *for me*, Jonas thought. *What the fuck am I going to do when Max finds out?* was the second thought that raced through his mind.

Jonas knew one thing, that he had to tell Max and try to stop all of this, but then he couldn't stop anything, it was done, and she had signed an agreement with Christian.

"What the fuck?" Jonas murmured, as he turned away from the lawyer sitting next to him, trying to get some sleep before the next rich asshole called with an emergency.

So, what was left for Jonas to do now? All he knew was Max had to know the truth. He had to get to the hotel and call him, and hope that Max would answer, and take his calls.

WHEN JONAS STEPPED out of the limo, into the hotel, and into the elevator, and opened the door of the suite, Maximillian was standing waiting to see who would walk through those doors.

"You look like shit, Jonas, where the fuck have you been and where's Alex? Where is she?" Max questioned, to Jonas's surprise.

Jonas didn't expect Max to be standing there, and the look on Jonas's face with his furrowed brow and large eyes signaled to Max that something had to be wrong, but he needed to hear it from Jonas first. Was it Alex again? Did someone who had a problem with him or Jonas do something to her? He couldn't go through this again, and he hated himself for exposing her to all Jonas's and his craziness.

Jonas needed time to relax, and try to modify the story, then he would call Max and explain to him over the phone, but now that idea was shot to hell. Jonas took a deep breath and then exhaled.

"Alex is no longer your wife, and you are to blame for that. If you didn't—"

"I don't need you to lecture me on what I did wrong, I take full responsibility for being a dick and a fool, but you're responsible too, Jonas," Max barked, and strolled over to get a drink from the hotel fridge. He twisted the top off, and emptied the small bottle of liquor into a glass and drank it.

Jonas didn't know what to say. He didn't know how to break the news to Max. He needed a drink too, because he didn't know how Max would react once he told him the whole story, but he needed a clear head first.

"You haven't told me where Alex is. I had my pilot turn the plane around because I finally realized that I would be nothing without Alex. I'm nothing. She saved me from myself and gave me my beautiful children," Max confessed, holding up a now empty glass. "The way I was going, not sleeping, and having to deal with all your shit, I almost lost my wife. I'm not blaming you because none of this would have happened if I hadn't placed a lot of responsibility on her shoulders."

Max downed that drink and was headed for another. "When I left last night—" Max didn't get a chance to continue before Jonas interrupted.

"You were here last night?"

"Yes, and where were you?"

"Max, do you mean you haven't read the papers, or listened to the news?"

"I didn't have time. I had to clear up some things with that industrial plant I still owned in Hong Kong, and sell it because it's too much of a headache. It's the reason I didn't have time for Alex and my children. Now I'm going to devote all my time to Alex, and we're going to take the children on a trip as a family. This might be the first time in our lives we're going on a vacation together." Max's eyes smiled along with the closed smile reaching up on both sides of his lips. It appeared that for once he was at peace with himself and contented.

Jonas watched Max fall into the sofa, and it appeared for the first time he'd seen his brother with such a broad smile, and it broke his heart, when he said, "Alex is no longer your wife."

"I know. I fucked up. However, if she accepts my marriage proposal, we can get married right away. I'm going to buy her another ring, the largest one I can find while I'm here in New York, and move her back to civilization." Max gushed with a brightness in his eyes which Jonas had never seen before, and he didn't want to be the one to take that light away, but he had to tell him.

Make him understand.

"I don't know how to say this... Alex married Christian Kenley tonight."

Max stared as if he couldn't understand the statement. He slanted his head and narrowed his glance as he aimed a glare at Jonas and began laughing. "You're joking, right? You just said that to punish me, right? I deserve to be punished, but not like that."

And then the color left Max's face. The wide smile disappeared from his exquisite features, and he wore a dour expression. His thick eyebrows rose, and his eyes narrowed and darkened.

When Jonas didn't break into a smile, Max's chest became heavy, and he realized that Jonas was serious. "Why the fuck would she do a thing like that when she knows how much I love her? Was she trying to get revenge when she married him? Tell me, Jonas, why would she marry a man like him?" He stepped closer to Jonas and Jonas stepped backward.

"Because of me," Jonas said in a small voice, hardly hearing his own words because he'd said those words so low.

"What the fuck do you mean because of you?" Max marched over to the fridge and poured another small bottle into his glass, and drank all of the liquor. Jonas got a glass and small bottle of Scotch in between Max talking about how much he loved Alex, and before Jonas broke the news. Jonas had been sipping on his glass of Scotch when he suddenly put it to his lips and swallowed it down.

Jonas turned to Max, "She did it for me," he admitted, his lips trembling and his words shaky.

"What did you say?" Max questioned breathlessly as he advanced in Jonas's direction.

Jonas held his breath, closed his eyes, and at that moment Max balled his fists at his sides. It took everything inside of him to gain control over his body, mind, and fist to keep from using them on his brother. Never would he have considered using his fists on Jonas, even as he'd given Max all the reasons for doing so. Max had never wanted to until now.

His love for his brother was as immense as his love for Alex.

Jonas walked back to the sofa, dropped down, and placed the glass on the table. He watched Max's solemn face and sour look, and Max's heavy feet trudged in the direction of the sofa and slowly Max sat down across from Jonas.

Jonas began to confess to Max how he'd gone to a club, met two pretty young girls who appeared to be twenty, but were in fact underage, and he'd been too drunk to know or care. He admitted that the girls asked him to go to a party, and he went because he wanted to get laid.

One girl hailed a taxi for them to take a short ride to an apartment in the village, and Jonas had gone up there with them to one of the girls' boyfriend's apartment.

Jonas told Max how he didn't remember what had happened to the young woman after he'd fucked her, or whether he did or not. He might have jacked off on her, and that was why she had his semen on her body.

Jonas went on to state to Max about how he didn't know how the woman died, or who brought her to the alley, and that she was a runaway. The police told Jonas that they'd identified her immediately when they arrested him, and after they'd found her. The police claimed later they did a DNA test, and found his semen on her body and clothes.

Max listened intently until Jonas had concluded the story.

They sat for hours without talking, or Max being accusatory of Jonas as he expected, but it never came. Finally, Max said, "I have to find Alex. Do you know where she is?"

"From what I understand from Christian's lawyer they're on his yacht."

"Then I'll find them no matter how long it takes." The look in Max's eyes scared Jonas and he wasn't easy to scare since this ordeal, however, lately Jonas had too many shocking experiences that just about wore him down, and he was at his breaking point.

"What are you going to do, Max?" Jonas questioned.

He'd never seen Max like this before. The look in his eyes, a faraway gaze terrified Jonas. He'd seen that one time before with Max when

Alex was kidnapped, and that episode with Robert, and it was anyone's guess what happened in Robert's apartment when Max was alone with him on Robert's final days.

Max reached for his phone and called his driver, "Meet me out front in three minutes." And he shoved his phone in his pocket and glanced over at Jonas and answered his question.

"What do you think I'm going to do? All I ask of you is that you don't get into any more fucking trouble until I return. I need you to go home, and take care of my children. I hope you can do that without any problems. I don't need any more worries and headaches. Do you understand?" Max turned and headed for the door.

Jonas followed Max to the door, and before Max stepped outside, Jonas's breath hitched, and he said, "Bring Alex back, will you?"

"Those are my intentions," Max said with a low ominous voice, and he closed his eyes for a second, turned away, and left Jonas standing by the open door.

The End for Now

Next book in the Blackstone Saga "Black Swan" book 9 and Blackout Book 10. Coming in 2024 Book 11 "Black Ice"

Don't miss out!

Visit the website below and you can sign up to receive emails whenever Rachel E Rice publishes a new book. There's no charge and no obligation.

https://books2read.com/r/B-A-ASU-NXIHB

BOOKS 2 READ

Connecting independent readers to independent writers.

Did you love *Black Tide*? Then you should read *Back to Black*[1] by Rachel E Rice!

[2]

When Maximillian Blackstone accused his twin brother of causing trouble in his family, and especially with his wife Alex who appeared to have a special and unusual bond with Jonas, there may have been some truth to Max's notion, but he made the mistake of voicing it to Jonas. Jonas realized that it was time to leave the security and protection of his big brother, especially since Max made it clear that he didn't want him around his wife Alex.

Jonas an army veteran of several tours in Afghanistan, finds himself alone in Florida, with no family, plenty of money and time, but no one to love and love him.

---

1. https://books2read.com/u/47rEn8

2. https://books2read.com/u/47rEn8

In Jonas's search for that one woman to love him, he'd been pulled back into a BDSM lifestyle he'd left. It was the lifestyle that made him feel alive especially since he'd thought he'd met the woman of his dreams.

Will this woman be able to replace Alex in his mind and his fantasies? Will she offer him a chance to heal his broken soul, or destroy him?

Read more at www.rachel-e-rice.com.

Also by Rachel E Rice

Blackstone
The Incredible Mr. Black
Blackstone Complete 10 Books Dark Romance Series
Temptation In Black
Blackstone Series 4 Books Box Set
Submission To Black
Black Tie Affair
The Incredible Mr. Black Box Set
Mourning Becomes Black
Fade To Black
Back to Black
Black Tide
Black Swan
Blackout
Blackstone Series 6 Books Box Set

I Am The Night
I Am The Night

Insatiable

Insatiable: The Lone Werewolf finds his mate
Insatiable: A Werewolf's Hunger
Insatiable: A Werewolf's Wedding
Insatiable: The Werewolves' Challenge
Hunter's Moon
Moon Tide
Moon Rapture

Insatiable Werewolf Series
A Bride For A Werewolf: The Beginning
Thorn in Moonscape
Insatiable: Damon in Moonscape
A Werewolf's Passion
Moonscape Box Set

Night
I Am First Night
I Am Last Night

Obsession
Obsession: Warm Bodies,Cold Hearts
Naked Obsession
Burning Obsession

Seduction
Seduced By An Earl

About the Author

Rachel E. Rice enjoys writing in different genres. As an Indie author she explores genres to find her voice. She has written contemporary romance, erotic romance, new adult, historical and science fiction.

When she's not writing she is reading poetry. She has a BA and is a member of Romance Writers of America.

Read more at www.rachel-e-rice.com.